JACKIRON

JACKIRON

A Caribbean Adventure

ROBERT WALLACE HUDSON

SHERIDAN HOUSE

First published 2001 by
Sheridan House Inc.
145 Palisade Street
Dobbs Ferry, NY 10522

Library of Congress Cataloging-in-Publication Data
Hudson, Robert Wallace
    Jackiron : a Caribbean adventure / Robert Wallace Hudson.
        p. cm.
    ISBN 1-57409-133-6 (alk. paper)
    1. West Indies—Description and travel. 2. Hudson, Robert Wallace,
1928– I. Title.
    F1613 .H83 2001
    917.2904'52—dc21

                                                                2001034389

Edited by Janine Simon
Designed by Jeremiah B. Lighter

Printed in the United States of America

ISBN   1-57409-133-6

Contents

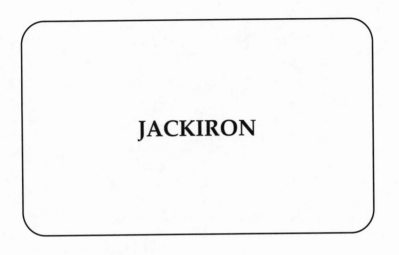

JACKIRON

CHAPTER 1

Flying to Puerto Rico

From high up on the mountainside looking over the trees I could see the sun just rising above the low rolling hills to the east. To the north, a dark cloud seemed attached to the high peaks, raining on the forest continually. Over to the left it was raining, and to the right, a glorious sunshine. Every day was the same. The sun's rays sparkled off wet foliage, danced about through the branches of scarlet flamboyant trees; the gracious scent of the frangipani and the view left one elated, excited.

I glanced down onto the rusty tin roofs of St. George's, a squalid little harbor town that played such a large role in Caribbean history. The roofs blended with the colorful painted buildings, the lustrous green foliage and a muddled humanity, most milling around, some hurrying.

There were forts and cannon platforms high up on the mountainside overlooking the harbor and I was standing on one. These bastions protected the town from sea attack during the French and English wars. Today, several of the old gun sites have been converted into fine homes.

I'm a civil engineer and a sailor, I was born in Georgia; my wife, Kate, is from Iceland. We met while I was working at Keflavik Airport; and now we were living in an apartment which had been built on one of these old emplacements, high above the town. From our patio we could see for fifty miles, give or take a little; on a clear day we could clearly identify islands in the Grenadines group, forty miles away.

I left the patio and went inside to gather my things for the trip to Puerto Rico; this was the day. I had to go ahead and get this damn thing over with. Maria must know what had happened.

Robin Williams, a commercial pilot friend of mine, had told me the week before that he would be flying up to Puerto Rico in a few days and I could get a lift. Robin had been giving me lessons in his twin-engine Apache. He had called the day before and asked if I could leave the next morning. I said, "Sure."

We took off about nine and set a course for San Juan, Puerto Rico. He let me fly the plane so I could build up hours; I needed a few more under his supervision and then I'd have a license for a twin-engine plane. Robin was a sneaky instructor, always kidding around. He and his wife Joan, and a new baby, had been making their home on the island of St. Vincent for about five years. He was in his early thirties, a bit chunky. Being British, he got a kick out of fooling me, a Yank. In the air, he could shut down an engine on me and I don't think I ever knew how he did it. Robin would pull the trick and then sit back and smile, which amounted to an ear-to-ear, closed mouthed grin, eyes wide open; he had quite a sense of humor. Flying a twin is the simplest thing in the world; it's like handling two single-engine planes at once. What you must learn is how to control it on one engine.

Robin and I had been in the air about thirty minutes when I felt the left rudder ease off, a tell-tale sign that one engine had quit.

"The port engine is down! Did you do it?" I glared at him.

"Hell, no!" He always lied. "Better check this, Captain. What do you see?" he asked.

"I see plenty of gas in that wing and the oil pressure is good. Prop's spinning, that's good, mag's fine. You did it, right?" I asked again.

He never admitted doing it, never. When the instructor pulls this stunt for the first time, it's scary.

"Try it now," Robin said calmly.

Starting that hot engine wasn't easy. Sometimes it would give you trouble; that's why it's essential for the student to learn to fly a twin on one engine.

But the engine started and my nervous system settled down.

There were numerous rainsqualls all around and we were weaving in and out of them, sometimes feeling the up drafts of wind associated with these huge thunderheads. Suddenly, between the clouds, I could see Aves Island (Bird Island) ahead, so I said, "Let's circle and see if there are any turtles on the beach." Aves Island is a tiny sand spit a hundred miles out in the Caribbean Sea. Thousands of female sea turtles come ashore there each year to lay their eggs.

"Okay."

"Did you read about the Englishman who was lost here two years ago?"

"I remember something. What happened?" he asked.

"Kate, my wife, and I were in Castries, St. Lucia, and a local schooner came in with a load of live turtles, which they sold in no time for a great big twenty-seven cents a pound, dressed. That was disgusting enough. An Englishman, cruising the world in a 45-foot yawl, was there. He decided catching turtles was a way to make good money, so he sent his wife and child ashore, removed the furnishing from the interior of the yacht, and sailed for Aves. When he got there, a native schooner was already gathering turtles. The captain told him he had heard on the radio that a hurricane was headed in this direction and suggested for him to get out. The Englishman said he'd gone to too much trouble to quit then. So he began to catch turtles. Now, these creatures will weigh eighty to one hundred and fifty pounds! It's a lot of work for a man to handle one alone.

"The captain of the schooner then made a fatal mistake. He offered for his young nephew to stay and help the Englishman. The schooner sailed away, leaving the two behind.

"Hurricane Beulah, as you will recall, passed over the Leeward Islands, and went into the Caribbean gaining speed, hitting Aves with 80-mile an hour winds. When it was obvious the Englishman was lost, another yacht went looking for the boat. All that could be found was the anchor and twenty fathoms of anchor chain lying on the bottom where he'd last been. It's my belief that he let the chain and anchor loose and tried to run before the storm. When the wind becomes too strong, such as in a hurricane, it's impossible to winch in the chain and anchor. After that, the boat began to pitch and roll violently, and the turtles he had caught had the last laugh. Live turtles are stored on board upside down, so they'll stay in one place. Well, the creatures, with their slick shells, began to slide back and forth as the yacht rolled, hitting the sides of the boat, until it finally broke apart and the turtles escaped back to the sea. The Englishman's wife and daughter were stranded in St. Lucia, penniless. Nothing was ever found of the men or the vessel."

The port rudder eased off again, and I said with some hostility, "Dammit, Robin! You did it again. Cut out the horseshit."

Robin jerked erect and shouted "What? I didn't do anything, Bob! Is the port down?"

"Yes, you bastard. It's down."

"Let me see, bloody hell."

He took over the controls and went through the engine-down checklist. "I think it's the port mag. It's been giving me trouble; I'll let her cool a bit, then try. I can always use the starboard magneto by switching over, you understand that?" Robin was very jittery.

"What are you so jumpy about? You pull this on me all the time!"

"I'll let you in on a little secret, the reason for this trip to San Juan is to have the starboard engine over-hauled, that one . . ." He pointed to the good engine, or should we say the engine that was still running.

"Now I know why you're giving me a free trip. You need me to help paddle the rubber dinghy. Some friend!"

Robin tried the starter, nothing. He switched magne-tos; nothing happened, I was beginning to feel sweaty and uncomfortable. The engine refused to start.

Robin said, "Let's give her a while and try again."

"You're the boss."

"Okay, here's what we'll do. Drop down to three thousand feet and lean her back 'til she's just flying, fuel and air mix for minimum consumption. All right, trim her out, we just might make it."

I said, "What the hell are you jabbering about, just make it! I thought we had everything under control."

"Flying with one engine uses more gas, dumb-dumb. I have no way to use the gas in the port wing. I think we'll have just barely enough."

The motor refused to start. I heard every stroke that starboard engine made all the way to Puerto Rico, but we finally saw the island in the distance and all was well again. Robin called in to the tower and asked if we could make a straight-in approach. The controller said there was no other traffic in the area, so come on in.

"Can you land her?" Robin asked.

"Sure, no problem." I was sitting in a puddle of sweat.

Robin and I landed at San Juan airport and since it was late, we got a couple of rooms in an out of the way bed and breakfast. Casa Mirabel was a grand private home a few years ago, but now it is a small, comfortable place for folks to rest. We had dinner and walked around the Old San Juan part of town. Finding a bar, we settled in for some serious drinking.

"I know it's none of my business, Bob, but I'm really curious. What are you up here for?" Robin asked.

I sighed, thinking of the ordeal ahead of me. "Well, it's a long story. You sure you want to hear it?" I replied.

"Yeah, I'm not the least bit sleepy, are you?"

"Okay, don't say I didn't warn you." I began. "It all started back in December when I got this call from Paul Watson in Grenada . . ."

CHAPTER 2

A Job Offer

The sea was rough. At our speed the little sports fishing boat was throwing spray 50 feet on either side. I would feel a whole lot better about this trip if the weather wasn't so dreadful. Damn, homesick already. Sure could use a rum and coke. My skin was itchy. Was this an onslaught of delirium tremens? No, just the dengue fever coming back. Don't forget your promise to Kate; no drinking on this trip.

I must have dozed off. It took me a minute to realize that I was on my way to Trinidad to take charge of an offshore supply ship. Glancing at my watch told me that we'd left St. George's over two hours ago.

Having gone broke in the yacht charter business, I'd sold my 86-foot schooner and I was out of work and bored. I found myself listless and depressed. My confidence, even my self-esteem, were shattered. Needless to say, my money was being used up at a reckless rate. Regardless, Kate, my wife, and I were living ashore in a luxurious apartment high up on the mountainside overlooking the harbor of St. George's, Grenada.

While I was enjoying a leisurely breakfast of papaya with passion fruit juice as a chaser, the phone rang. Paul Watson, a West Indian who had several businesses in Grenada and was a friend of mine, asked if I would be interested in skippering a 132-foot supply ship to the Dominican Republic, where I would pick up and deliver a well drilling outfit to Basse-Terre, Guadeloupe.

"Wow, let me wake up before you hit me like that." But after thinking about it for a second or two, I said, "Maybe, if the money is right."

"The trip should take ten or twelve days and it's worth a thousand bucks to you, " Paul said.

"U.S. money?" I asked, thinking a hundred bucks a day wasn't bad.

"Yes," was the reply.

The last couple of months I'd been so lethargic, a sea trip sounded like a cure. It'd get me out of the house and, besides, I might lose some weight. Maybe even get back in shape. Kate, my beautiful wife of eleven years, who was listening to the conversation, said, "Why not, we could use the money." So it was agreed, as long as I promised to be back by Christmas.

Paul said, "If you can make it, we'll leave this afternoon on Jimmy Stilwell's fishing boat."

He came by to pick me up around noon. We were leaving at two-thirty. I said, "Have lunch with us before we leave, Paul. Have a drink and tell me everything."

Paul was a white West Indian, tall, about six-two, a little soft around the waist, but weren't we all. His home was in Trinidad, but most of his businesses were in Grenada—hotel, marina and other things I didn't know about. Paul was the kind of man who dabbles in a lot of ventures, hoping at least one will make him rich. At that time, he was dabbling, but not too rich.

"Who owns the vessel?" I asked.

"Malcolm Coma, he's a friend of mine," Paul said. " From San Fernando, in the salvage and underwater repair business."

"What kind of shape is this boat in?" I asked.

"Malcom's got several. I don't know which one he intends using," he replied.

"Well, what can you tell me about his operation? It's my ass going out on his ship."

"Bob, don't expect too much, and you won't be disappointed," Paul replied. "I haven't been by his yard in San Fernando for at least two years."

"You lying asshole, give me back that drink." I made like I was going to kick him. "If you sell me down the river, Kate will scratch out them lyin' eyes. Won't you, hon?"

Over lunch, I was unable to get Paul to expand on his knowledge of Malcolm Coma's operation. We were eating Kate's special lobster salad: celery, spring onions, eggs, mayonnaise, whipped cream, a little mustard and limejuice. Of course lobster, served with avocado on a bed of lettuce. I even threatened to take his food away, but he still wouldn't tell me anymore. This made me suspicious, but not enough to call off the trip.

After lunch we went down to the marina and I met Jimmy, Paul's fishing buddy, another Trinidadian who'd just spent a week fishing for marlin and sail fish. We boarded Jimmy's sports fishing boat, and soon we were on our way to Trinidad. Jimmy, our skipper, was a young white West Indian, heavy set, but all muscle. He was very business-like till he started drinking, then he became the life of the party. So I was told.

I sat in the fighting chair of a 28-foot sports fisherman. Paul and the skipper were up on the flying bridge. The little ship was tearing along at sixteen to eighteen knots, depending on whether we were going up the face of the swells or plunging down the other side. It was a rough ride any way you cut it. The little boat left the water at the top of each wave and slammed down on the other side, and my kidneys complained bitterly. The sea was running high, four- to six-foot swells coming in from the direction of Africa and two- to three-foot wind waves on top of the swells. That was enough to take the edge off anyone's appetite.

I was trapped in the chair in the cockpit, alone, seemingly the only person left on the globe. The boat was flying around so much, I couldn't have moved if I'd wanted to. It was eerie; with the spray and the noise, I was in some sort of torture chamber. I needed a rum and coke bad. I just had to hang on!

Swiveling the chair around forward, I could barely make out the tops of the mountains on Trinidad, about forty miles off. I gazed aft at the snowy whiteness of our churning wake against the dirty gray of the sea, the same color as the sky. From force of habit I looked up. The overcast clouds were threatening. Here and there were black thunderheads building in intensity; sooner or later they would unleash their ferocity on land or sea.

I looked around for any low clouds that might dump on us. There it was, to windward about two to three miles, a maverick low in the sky. A storm so close it seemed to be connected to the sky and the sea at the same time. Underneath, I could clearly see the white on the wave tops being blown to leeward by the fierce winds. It didn't take a weatherman to tell me this was it. The storm was a couple of miles wide and no more than five hundred feet off the water. And we were on a collision course with it!

I swiveled the chair around again and tried to catch the attention of the guys on the bridge. Finally, sticking my fingers between my teeth, I whistled, pointing to the thunderstorm, and they nodded. I wondered what Jimmy would do. I hoped he had enough experience to do the right thing. Being a pro will get you in trouble sometimes, some people resent other people's advice. I thought, this is his boat, hold your peace. But I knew he should slow down or stop to let the storm go ahead of us.

Instead, Jimmy decided he could outrun the storm. Little did he know the thunderheads were traveling at twenty-five to thirty knots and we were doing half that. It's surprising how quickly these squalls can be on top of a boat. One minute you think, hey, I'm gonna beat this, and the next, the full fury hits. The wind first, then the rain blowing horizontally, stinging so bad you can't look to windward. That doesn't matter anyway, because there's nothing to see.

Within seconds, visibility was cut to zero. The waves were thrown up and suddenly the vessel was nearly out of control. All that the man at the helm can do is hang on and hope. Thank goodness, he'd cut back the engines. In a sailing ship caught with its sails up, this is a bad time. Heavy squalls have frightened me many times, especially on dark nights.

The thunderhead passed; the worst was over, and in a couple of minutes we could see again. It was still raining hard and the wind was up, but we were past the danger. After a while the sun came out, and the world looked good again.

I must have dozed off because when I woke up we were in the Coca-Cola colored water that surrounds Trinidad. Just south of the island is the mouth of the huge Orinoco River. Second only to the Amazon in size around here, the river comes out of the dense jungles and spews its dark brown waters up and down the coast for miles. Trinidad is completely surrounded by this discolored waters. When a ship approaches the island from the sea, often the captain knows where he is by the color of the water.

The small ship entrance to the Gulf of Paria, our destination, is between the mainland and an island called Monos. This entrance is called Bocas or Boca. I never knew which. We would be arriving after dark and I hoped our skipper knew the way through, because there were no navigation lights to assist him.

We finally arrived in calm water. Jimmy, the captain, idled the engines and climbed down from the flying bridge. He was young, in his early twenties, and reminded me of a line backer. He lifted the engine hatches and checked the level of the water in the bilge.

"Hey, we got water, lots of it," he said.

It didn't take long for the electric pump to clear the water out, and soon we were off again. While the hatches were open, I took a quiet, professional look at his engine room. It was immaculate, no rust, dirt or any of the usual stuff.

"Congratulations, that's a fine looking engine room," I said.

"I don't do it. I have a guy that does nothing but spruce up this little baby," he said.

"Not bad, not bad at all," I said.

After his carelessness during the storm, he was smart to check the engines. The stern glands were leaking badly and the bilge was half full of water. Each propeller shaft passes through the stern glands, which in turn must pass through the hull. The sea water cools the glands made of rubber, and in rough seas more water comes in than is needed. He took a turn on the greasers that will hold about a quarter cup and are designed to fill the glands with grease and slow the leaks down.

While we were sitting there in the relatively quiet waters behind the island, I looked across the channel into Plymouth Bay, a small, natural inlet that was completely deserted. I could hear a troop of howler monkeys settling in for the night. The darkness was filled with their loud, low hoots, grunts and screeches. To the average person, the noise sounds like there are hundreds of monkeys, but in reality a troop consists maybe of only ten or fifteen animals.

On my first trip to Trinidad a couple of years earlier, I'd decided to stop in Plymouth. It was nearly dark and I didn't like the idea of approaching Port of Spain at night, with all its off-lying dangers. We motored in and anchored about a hundred yards offshore. The bay was very quiet and deserted, so we all had a good night's sleep, but just before dawn, we were suddenly awakened by an incessant, blood chilling noise. I thought, maybe we're being attacked by Carib Indians! I ran up on deck and found the terrified crew huddled together.

"What the hell is that racket?" I asked.

"We don't know," was the reply.

"Look yonder!" shouted Winston, a West Indian from the island of Bequia. He was pointing toward the jungle.

Large, noisy, furry animals were moving through the jungle, leaving a 30-foot path of destruction in their wake. The howlers were on their way to breakfast. The crew were very agitated and I heard someone say, "Oh Lord, what have we got into!"

"Calm down, it's only monkeys," I shouted.

Suddenly, with an equally terrifying sound, hundreds of black vultures took wing and rose up from the low foliage. The sky and the sun were eclipsed by this mass of scavengers taking flight.

The boys were down on their knees with their arms up over their heads to ward off the imminent attack. I must confess, I was also pretty frightened.

The bay was finally quiet and we all sat around on deck, waiting for breakfast, telling each other, "I wasn't scared, were you scared?"

During World War II, the U.S. Navy had built a sub-chaser base there in Plymouth Bay. Now, all that remained were the steel frames of the prefab buildings the

Navy boys lived in. The sheet metal siding and roofs had long gone, but because of their strength, these metal joists were used as roosting places for the vultures. Just at dusk, hundreds of them converged on the old building skeletons, squawking, pushing, and complaining. It would be hard to believe, but if you were trapped there, you could survive. There really was no danger.

A while later, I asked the crew, just young guys, "Who would like to go ashore and look around?" I had no takers.

That was my first visit to this island.

Trinidad is known for its foliage, which is different from any of the other West Indian islands because it is only thirty or forty miles from South America. Over the millenniums, birds dropped seeds and propagated most of the plants found on the mainland. Some animals drifted across the channels on logs and such. Still, I'd never heard of panthers or other beasts of prey being found on the island. There are numerous species of birds that fly back and forth as they please. All the other islands of the West Indies have very few animals and birds. The importation of the dreaded mongoose, a nasty little bugger, took care of that.

During our first vacation to Trinidad, we met Asa Wright, a locally famous person. Mrs. Wright was deeply involved in preserving the environment of the island. Her late husband had been a great lawyer back in England. When he contracted a crippling disease, they had moved to Trinidad and built a beautiful home in the mountains overlooking Port of Spain. After her husband's death, Mrs. Wright gave the estate to the government, and it was developed as a Nature Park. She was allowed to live there for life, the government maintaining the house and park.

Through mutual friends she learned that Kate was from Iceland and, being Icelandic herself, she wanted to meet her. We were invited for lunch. On the appointed day we were waiting on the dock when around the corner came a vintage limousine: chauffeur in front, Asa Wright in back. She turned out to be one of the nicest ladies we'd ever met. The Nature Park was also very interesting, every flower, shrub and flowering tree indigenous to Trinidad was exhibited. The lunch was fabulous: callaloo (a green leaf vegetable) soup, sauteed mountain chicken (frog legs) in a wine sauce and a green salad.

We were taken down into some caves where we saw the very rare oily birds. This small bird is near extinction, and we were fortunate enough to see some of the last to survive. In the 1800s, these birds were actually set on fire to provide light. Hence the name oily bird, as they are a very fatty creature.

Finally, the little sports fishing boat was inside the Gulf of Paria. I could see the lights of Port of Spain and, further down the coast, the lights of San Fernando, our final destination.

CHAPTER 3

A Rusty Old Hulk

Jimmy, our skipper, knew his home waters well. He made it to the dock in San Fernando without mishap, arriving at about eight-thirty. I found out that he belonged to the wealthy elite of this small, impoverished island. After the formalities with Customs and Immigration were over, we found a local bar and had a beer while Jimmy told us about his hobbies.

Other than sports fishing, he liked spearing grouper in the dark brown waters of the Gulf of Paria. In the old days, the Gulf was one of South America's largest oil producers, with scores of oil drilling rigs dotting its waters. Now the rigs were gone, as was the oil. All that remained were hundreds of old pilings, large wooden posts that held up the drilling platforms. Giant grouper, some weighing up to four hundred pounds, thrived around these old posts, and Jimmy and his friends would dive into the dark waters and literally feel for a grouper. Once found, the fish was shot with a spear, a stout line attached.

"This is where the fun begins," Jimmy related. "A 400-pound fish is hard to handle! After the fish is speared and secured, I bring the line back to the boat where it's made fast to a strong cleat. The grouper is then allowed to thrash around till it's tired out. Later, the line is attached to a block and tackle on the gin pole, and then the fish is hoisted up and into the cockpit of the boat. Me and the guys that play this game have many a scar from past battles with those monsters."

"Now don't get the idea this sort of adventure happens very often," Jimmy assured me. "It doesn't, we might go out and spend days before finding a fish, we're feeling for grouper in dark water. We ain't pros, so we sell the fish wholesale to pay for new diving equipment: spears, nylon line, beer, other things. Last July a 420-pound fish near 'bout drowned me; my arm got caught up in the spear line. That fish had me under for about three minutes before I could cut the line. But we got him in the end."

The Gulf of Paria is huge, some sixty to seventy miles in diameter, with Venezuela to the west and Trinidad to the east. Volcanic explosions created the Gulf, archaeologists say.

Trinidad has two things going for it—oil and tourism. This makes her the most advanced island in all the British West Indies. Unfortunately, little of these riches ever reach the common people. The few wealthy families live outside of town on their plantations or estates, far from the dirt and squalor of Port of Spain. Still, there is a small but growing middle class, consisting of typists, salesmen and clerks. Secretaries usually come from the upper middle class, and a few from the rich, giving the girls a chance to get out and meet some of the young professionals. But the line drawn between the various classes is as solid as the Berlin Wall used to be. It is possible for a woman to go from the lower class to the lower middle class, but it takes a lot of good looks and hard work.

The next day I met Malcolm A. Coma, the owner of the supply ship for which I was to be responsible. He was in his late thirties or early forties, about five foot ten, with wide shoulders like a boxer. Malcolm was French, from the island of Martinique, and had lived in Trinidad for many years, making his living as a professional diver. His company, MACCO, accepted all the underwater repair jobs around the offshore oil rigs that no one else would do. Working on a shoestring, he didn't, or wouldn't, observe the normal safety rules, even though working without proper gear and equipment might mean death to his divers. Just the week before I arrived, his brother-in-law had drowned while working at a depth of only fifty feet. Some say it was faulty equipment that caused the accident.

It was easy to tell Malcolm was French, with his straight black hair, square jaw, and narrow nose, few of the features of the English West Indian. He used his initials to name his fleet of vessels. The ship I was to command was called MACCO 17. At the time, MACCO 17 was working on the other side of the island at the main onshore oil terminal. This terminal, with its huge storage tanks, received oil pumped from the oil drilling rigs located fifteen or twenty miles offshore, in the Atlantic. The oil was then transferred to ocean-going tankers that took it to refineries around the world.

Malcolm and I drove over the mountains on our way to the terminal, through the many truck farms that grew everything from pineapples to yams. Trinidad has two main groups of people, the West Indians, whose ancestors were brought in as slaves, and the East Indians, who were brought from India to the island as indentured laborers many years ago. The people of Trinidad say the East Indians are their gardeners. Over the years, they have acquired a large percentage of the tillable land. Malcolm and I passed through several copra (coconut) plantations, banana plantations and even a rain forest. In the rain forest, the vegetation is thick and green, and always wet; it looks artificial. The birds of Trinidad are extremely colorful, especially the macaw, with its plumage of red, yellow and several shades of green, and are so easily spotted against the deep lustrous greens of the forest cloak. It's a lush and beautiful island once you are away from the squalid towns.

As Malcolm and I approached the terminal, it was obvious this was a first class operation. The harbor was manmade and was large enough to handle huge ocean-going tankers. The place smelled of crude oil, which I dislike intensely. But, some people say it smells of money. This harbor is one of those places you want to see once and then leave fast. The guard at the gate checked Malcolm's pass and told him, "Mr. Coma, Captain Higgins, the harbormaster, gave me instructions to tell you he must see you immediately." Malcolm grunted and glanced at me; I guessed something wasn't right by the look on his face, but I had no idea just what.

So far I'd been smiling. But once we pulled up beside a rusty old hulk, however, my smile quickly faded with disbelief. Lying alongside the jetty was the oldest, ugliest, rustiest ship I had ever laid eyes on, surely on its way to the salvage yard. There was more corrosion on her than paint and from bow to stern there were endless indentations as if a giant Gulliver had wheeled a one-ton hammer over and over again.

"Is this it?" I asked, not trying to hide my dismay and disappointment.

"What did you expect?" Malcolm said with no emotion.

"Damn, she looks a mess," I said. "She just won't do."

"Hey, wait till you get the feel of her before you make any snap decisions," Malcolm said.

The harbormaster, Mr. Higgins, drove up and

wasted no time in informing Malcolm, "Mr. Coma, you have thirty minutes to get your vessel out of my harbor or I'll cut her lines. Do you understand me?"

Malcolm was obviously accustomed to this sort of treatment. He nodded, unconcerned, and called his skipper over. Sidney, a chubby East Indian in his early thirties, was given instructions to move the vessel back to the base in San Fernando. I watched as the crew, two blacks and two East Indians, took her out of the harbor. They seemed to work well together and it wasn't long before the ship was slipping past the harbor entrance and heading out into the open sea.

I was ready to go, but Malcolm had cornered Mr. Higgins. He was asking, in a most humbling manner, for better treatment. The harbormaster, a polite but impatient Englishman, said he didn't like Malcolm's vessels using the harbor for day-to-day moorings. He reminded him that it was a place for tankers and said Malcolm would have to do like everyone else and move the ship back into Port of Spain when the work was over.

Riding back to San Fernando in the truck with Malcolm, I began thinking of some way that I could get out of this situation. Common sense said, run!

I had sold my schooner after going broke in the charter business, along with a lot of other yacht owners, mainly because the smaller, more modern bareboat fleets had taken over from our larger, so-called luxurious sailing yachts. Maybe I was to blame, too. It's common knowledge here in the Caribbean that almost everyone in the charter business drank too much. Still, it was terrific while it lasted. And wasn't our motto, "Just another shitty day in paradise?" After I sold the yacht, Kate and I had moved ashore on Grenada and tried to live the good life.

I needed to do something to build my confidence, to prove to myself and to others that I could do it. Was I a damn fool? This was no sea-going vessel. It was an old, worn out, coastal supply ship, not fit to go on any long sea voyage. On the other hand, if the hull was tight and the equipment okay. . . . Oh, hell, I might do it, I thought to myself.

Finally, I said to Malcolm, "I expected a seaworthy vessel. Christ, your ship looks like a wreck. I have no intention of drowning on this trip, or any other. Malcolm, if I go, and that's a big if, I'll need eighty bucks a day till the trip is over."

"Check the vessel out, and you tell me if it's seaworthy," Malcolm said. "I'll leave it up to you, and as far as the money goes, I'll pay you seventy-five, tops."

Finally we agreed.

Around three o'clock that afternoon the ship anchored in the bay at San Fernando. When the crew finally came ashore, I asked the skipper, "What took you so long?"

"Her bottom's dirty," Sidney replied. "She needs hauling out, cleaning and painting real bad." Sidney was a slightly overweight six-footer Hindu with a mahogany complexion. Later I learned that he was a family man, and had four young children. He did not drink, nor did he smoke.

"How are the engines?" I asked.

"They were rebuilt a couple of years ago, I'd say they're okay. Better ask George, the engineer. He's been around for years. If anybody knows those engines, he does."

Sidney and I walked over to where George was cleaning some pump parts and I introduced myself.

"George, I'm Bob Hudson, and I'll be in charge on this trip north."

George, a small man with jet-black skin, looked me

straight in the eyes and said, "I don't know if I'll be going with you, Cap."

My mouth fell open; I stood back and had a look at this man who had the nerve to go up against his boss and refuse to do his job. George did not have a shirt on; his lean body was shining with sweat and all his sinuous muscles were rippling in the sun as he strained on the engine parts.

This really shocked me. If the only person who knew the ins and outs of the engine room wasn't going, neither was I. On older ships, things such as pipe markings, valve identification, and pump instructions are lost in poorly maintained engine rooms. You really have to know your engine room to make things work. For this one reason, it was absolutely essential for George to go with us. There was no way we could hire a new man and get him trained in time to do the trip.

"Does Mr. Coma know about this?" I asked.

"Mr. Coma knows I don't like being away from home at night," George said.

"George, do me a favor. Go over and talk to Mr. Coma," I said. "Tell him what you just told me."

Malcolm, who was standing on the dock, spent about ten minutes talking with George, obviously reaching some understanding. George came over and told me he would go on the trip. I did not ask for an explanation.

But this made me wonder about the other crew. This voyage was a big deal. These men probably had never been away from home in their lives. Maybe I should have a meeting and find out more. But that was really Malcolm's job. If they went, then it would be for the whole trip; having to fly one or all of them back home was unthinkable.

I asked Malcolm, "What do I do if one of them

decides he's got to go home somewhere up the islands? I'm used to sailors; these guys ain't sailors."

"I told all of them you're the captain. Whatever's got to be done, you'll do it, and that I'd frown on the ones who don't finish the trip. You got four of the best; you can depend on them. Just show them what you want, they'll get it done," Malcolm replied.

"Malcolm, did you tell them how dangerous this trip could be?" I asked. He shrugged his shoulders and walked away.

Even after all this talk, my gut reaction was to walk away! I kept thinking, here I am starting out on a 2,000-mile voyage with a ship that was obviously not designed for ocean work and a crew that was not accustomed to life at sea. I wondered if maybe Malcolm had the ship heavily insured and considered us expendable. But who would insure this beat-up old barge, certainly not Lloyds of London.

I went back to the hotel and decided to call Kate, since she always has a clear view of things.

"Kate, I believe this is a poor deal, the ship is a mess and the crew are not experienced seamen. John and this guy Malcolm Coma are setting me up. Do you think I should tell them to piss off?"

"How is the hull, the engines?" she asked.

"I don't know, but I'll definitely find out."

"Honey child, you know your stuff. If you feel she won't make it, come on home, but if she will and the money's right, do it," she said.

"Well, that's about what I figured, I just wanted to hear it from someone besides myself."

"I'm always here to help. Take care, love. Call me every chance you get if you decide to go."

I hung up and lay back on the bed in my room and stared at the ceiling.

Finally, I walked down to the dock and found some of the crew standing around talking. I walked over to Sidney, "You're the skipper; this is your boat," I said. "Why don't you take it up to the Dominican Republic?"

"I've never been out of sight of land, Skip, I can't navigate," Sidney replied sheepishly, not looking me in the eyes. "Captain, we go home at night."

All the crew seemed fine now, but that could change in an instant. Some little incident, some word, then animosity. Could blacks, East Indians and a white captain get along while isolated onboard an old ship for days on end?

I went on board and continued my inspection of the vessel. In the engine room, which is below the deck and aft, I asked George, "How long have you been on this old boat?"

At first you didn't notice it because George usually kept his mouth shut, but he had the biggest smile you'd ever seen, and the whitest teeth. He flashed those teeth when he answered proudly, "Six years this March, Cap. I know this engine room like I know my own bed." The room was filled with equipment: two twelve-cylinder General Motors diesel engines, generators, pumps, miles of piping, all painted white and streaked with rust. Electrical wiring was hanging everywhere.

"Will the engines make this trip?" A question I could not answer.

"I'd like to have the injector tips replaced and the fuel pumps adjusted," George answered.

"How much to do one injector?"

"About fifty dollars each," George said.

Each engine has twelve cylinders, that's twenty-four at fifty each. "Will Mr. Coma go for twelve hundred dollars?" I asked.

"You ask him and see. He might," George replied.

I liked George, a dapper little man about fifty years old. He had muscular arms and a slim waist; I'd say he was in good physical shape. He always said what was on his mind and did his work without a lot of talk. I saw him leaving the boat one afternoon, all decked out in a dark blue pin-striped suit, black shirt and white tie, white and brown oxfords. I'd noticed he walked with a strut, raising up on the toes of his right foot as he strolled along. I knew I wanted this man on board with me. He had class.

After I completed my inspection of the ship, I went ashore, and Malcolm and I talked business.

"Malcolm, I'll go on the trip if you'll take care of a couple of things," I said.

"What's that?" he asked. He continued reading his newspaper, not showing much interest.

"Clean the bottom, and the injector tips must be replaced," I continued.

Without hesitation, Malcolm said, "I'll take care of it."

"Can I depend on you?"

"I'll start them cleaning the bottom, just now."

I walked back to town from the dock. I was staying in a small hotel in San Fernando called the Empire. In the old days, when Trinidad was part of the British Empire, this was the meeting place for the gentlemen of the Foreign Corps and the officers of His Majesty's Twelfth Lancers, or some such unit. The lobby was two stories high with huge windows, tall and narrow, and thick satin drapes from ceiling to floor. They were the colors of the empire: deep red, bluish purple, trimmed with gold, faded. They could have used a rest and a good cleaning. The wooden wainscot on each wall was in need of paint badly. The old paint—gold, I believe—was peeling and flaking off. My room had no toilet or bath; both were three or four doors down the hall. I did have a wash basin with cold water, which must have been installed as an afterthought twenty or thirty years earlier. Electricity went in about the same time.

At the bar that night I met an elderly couple from London. Mr. and Mrs. Smyth-Stewart were on holiday, revisiting the island for the first time in twenty-eight years. They had been stationed not too far from San Fernando toward the end of World War II. I told them I had lived aboard a boat on the Thames for six years.

They were amazed. Mr. Smyth-Stewart said, "We used to go down to Taggs Island on the river Thames and walk around admiring the yachts. One of our favorites was an American boat."

"Was it a 38-foot cruiser with a rebel flag off the stern?" I asked.

"It's a small world, isn't it, old chap?" the gentleman replied.

They invited me to accompany them on an afternoon trip to a huge swamp called the Savan, located between the town and the airport, home of the scarlet ibis. With the workers cleaning the bottom of the boat, I had the next day off. So I said to myself, why not?

We traveled by taxi to the nearest point next to the swamp, then rented a skiff with an outboard motor and a guide. By boat it was another forty-five minutes before we finally entered a very large open area, which we were told was the Savan. It was about a quarter of a mile in diameter, a shallow lake. Dry at low tide and underwater by six to twelve inches at high tide, it literally supported thousands upon thousands of birds—cranes, scarlet ibis, white ibis, herons, seagulls, and many more. There was an abundance of food in those brackish waters, small frogs, insects, fish, also their eggs.

At dusk, high in the sky, the various flocks began to gather, first just a few, then more and more until they resembled clouds swirling around. The sun was very low, and the birds, six to eight hundred feet in the air, picked

up the last of the sun's rays. The scarlet ibis were spectacular in their coming together, the sun reflecting off
their red wings as they circled. Suddenly, seemingly
without guidance, the flock turned, one or two birds at
first, then a steady stream forming into a shallow dive toward the mangrove trees that bordered the Savan. As the
birds landed on their favorite branches, the trees began
to take on the look of a fruit orchard, each tree covered
with either white or red birds. They did not mix and,
once they were in their trees, the noise was deafening,
like one squawking bird multiplied by thousands. After
only ten minutes or so, the sky was empty and all the
trees we could see were filled with birds. Quite a sight! It
was well worth the effort to get there. During all this
commotion, the smaller birds were quite happily feeding
in the shallow water all around our boat.

The next day I tried to see a little more. San Fernando is typically West Indian, loud, colorful, and dirty.
The marketplace comes alive on Saturdays, when people from all over the island come to sell their goods,
visit, talk, drink rum and go home in the evening with
a snoot full. Don't get me wrong, there are West Indians
who frown on rum drinking and such, but usually it's
the women in their white dresses who try to teach their
children right from wrong. These same women practice
obeah, a form of voodooism. For a price, usually ten or
fifteen dollars, you can hire an obeah man or woman
to sculpt you a wooden figurine representing your favorite enemy. You can then pierce the doll with pins
to cause your enemy severe pain, or even death, so
they say.

The people of Trinidad had long ago accepted inter-
marriages between blacks and whites, but the East Indians and Asians didn't. The island included the blacks
descended from slaves, the East Indians whose forefathers were brought over from India as indentured

laborers at the end of slavery, a few Asians, and the whites whose forefathers were the original landowners. I must not leave out the French heritage, which is hard to find, but nevertheless exists; it takes a search of the government archives to trace the history. The French conquered Trinidad from the Spanish but lost it in 1802 to the English during the Napoleonic wars. Trinidad had been part of the British Empire until just recently.

Throughout the marketplace women were cooking on charcoal-burning braziers, deep-frying polouri (chickpea fritters), sabinas (taro leaves coated with batter) and fish balls (my favorite is shark). This is good stuff, and the tourists love it.

Naturally, the African influence is pervasive throughout the West Indies, simply because they outnumber all other races. But East Indian and Oriental dishes are very popular, not just as ethnic food, but liked by the blacks as well. The national dish of Trinidad is pelau, which consists of chicken, rice, pigeon peas, saffron, raisins, tomatoes and occasionally red meat.

MACCO 17 lay close in shore, and I watched as a dozen or more men repeatedly dove down to clean the steel bottom of the vessel. There were at least two inches of barnacles on her bottom. The brown water, mixed with the silt from the nearby fields, was the color of *café au lait*. The divers could not see in this water and worked by touch only. Most of them suffered from numerous barnacle cuts; just brushing against the little brutes results in abrasions.

It took two days for the men to finish cleaning the bottom and for fuel and water to be pumped aboard. Malcolm personally brought the food stores down to the dock in the back of his pick-up. We loaded one hundred pounds each of rice, potatoes and red beans, fifty pounds of onions, three twenty-pound bolognas, six dozen eggs, twelve loaves of bread and enough coffee, sugar, butter, lard and dry milk to last us a good twenty days.

Malcolm did not replace the injectors.

"Bob, I've had some recent financial setbacks and I can't afford to do that work just now," he told me.

"If an engine goes bad, I'll have to pull into the nearest port!"

"Hey, I understand! If you have any trouble, call me."

We were all set to go.

CHAPTER 4

Leaving the Security of the Land

On December 10, 1972, at four o'clock in the afternoon, we backed away from the dock at San Fernando, heading north on our way to the Dominican Republic, eight hundred and twenty nautical miles away. On the dock before we left, the families of the crew were well represented: wives, children, relatives, a lot of folks were there to see us off. The women implored me to see that their husbands and their sons remained safe throughout the trip.

"Now you keeps him away from all those nasty ladies what's got Lord only knows, you hear me, Captain?"

"I understand, and I'll do my best, ma'am."

The crew consisted of Sidney, the regular skipper, an East Indian and devout Hindu. Sidney had the edge on the others when it came to brains. He was ten or fifteen pounds overweight, with a round face and a little potbelly. His main job was to pilot the ship, with the help of the others, maneuvering alongside or tying up to the offshore rigs.

George, the engineer, was an older black man of about fifty, who definitely had the respect of the other members of the crew. He was quiet and spoke softly with authority. He was about five-foot-five, one hundred-forty pounds of muscle. I would guess he might have had a couple of pounds of fat, at the most. His fingers, when we shook hands, were long and thick. He had always worked as a mechanic, and was very strong.

George's assistant, Robbie, was a young man of twenty-two. He, too, was East Indian and followed the Hindu religion. A bit shy and wide-eyed with the world, he was the ship's welder and assistance engineer. His slight build fooled you into thinking he was sickly, but on the contrary, Robbie could do more work than the rest.

Joseph was the deck hand and cook. He was a joker, a black man who loved to make fun of just about anything or anybody. He had more than his share of self-confidence, to say the least. Sometime in the past, Joseph had shaved his head, so the men called him *Baldhead*. He was tall, about six-foot-two, had strong features and a pleasant smile. He told me, "Cap, you can depend on me, I'll feed you (he was the ship's cook), fight for you, and fuck your women, if you let me." Then he laughed, "And that a guarantee."

"What's the guarantee I wouldn't open up your head?" I said. If he answers this wrong, I was thinking, he doesn't go with us on the trip.

"Don't take me serious, I didn't mean that last remark. I like to tease." He wasn't laughing now and I believed him.

"If you can cook and fight, me and you will get on just fine."

Malcolm hired an additional man called Pimp, who was known for working the sailors coming off the freighters in Port of Spain. He was of medium build, had a pockmarked face and a permanent frown. I asked Pimp what experience he had as a sailor, and his reply was anything but reassuring. "I yam what I yam," he said, flexing his biceps. It wasn't a very big arm and I was confused at his meaning. He must have been a Popeye fan.

Robbie did the welding when necessary. On this old tub, that would be considerable, just to keep her together. He was thin and quite shy; it took me a while to get him to say anything.

"Your name's Robbie? How long have you been on board?" I asked.

"Yes sir, I been here nearly a year."

"You like shipwork?"

"It's okay."

"You married? Got any kids?"

"No, sir."

Sidney was at the wheel. We were headed north for the Bocas, a small channel between the islands. My cabin was directly behind the wheelhouse or bridge, which was located atop the raised bow of the ship, about ten feet above the main deck. The main deck was approximately one hundred feet long, thirty feet wide, and about four feet above the waterline. There was a three-foot high steel bulwark that ran along each side for the length of the main deck, but it did not enclose the stern of the vessel. The crew's cabin was in the bow and under the wheelhouse on the main deck. It was about twenty feet wide and fifteen feet long, containing eight bunks, a galley with a propane gas stove, a toilet and shower, but no refrigerator! It had all the comforts of home, except for the refrigerator. And it was clean, sort of.

MACCO 17 was built in Texas some thirty years ago, so the story goes. I was worried: would she stand up to the open sea? Most ships have sharp pointed bows with a cutwater to knife through the seas. Well, old MACCO 17 had a bow as round as an apple, hence the name *apple-bowed*, and she would smash, rather than cut, her way through the waves. This was not good.

As we approached the Bocas, the sun was setting. The moon was in its last quarter, as thin as a fingernail, and would not rise till three or four in the morning. The night would be dark. We passed through the Bocas. Plymouth Bay looked ominous and unwelcoming. The howlers were fast asleep. We were headed out into the open sea. There was nothing, just empty space, dark and dreadful. It was so black we couldn't see the line of the horizon. We were leaving the security of the land and its snug harbors, our warm beds, our wives and children. I alone had experienced this moment before. It is never easy. You feel fear of the unknown. What if a great storm strikes, an uncontrollable leak floods the hull, or we collide with another ship in the night? What if we hit a floating mine left over from World War II? All these things could and do happen, and happen fast.

My mind drifted back to another moonless night, when I'd been sailing my schooner hard for hours through bad seas, really taking a beating. Brother King, my first mate, a West Indian from Bequia, had come from below and yelled, "Cap, the ship is flooded!" He was extremely excited and wanted to abandon ship right then and there. I had noticed the bows were plunging into the waves more than usual, but it hadn't dawned on me something was wrong. I rushed below to see for myself and found a foot or so of water in the bilge forward. Fortunately, we were within five or six miles of St. Vincent and it didn't take long to get us into calm waters. Later, we were forced to bale the ship out with five-gallon buckets, because someone had stored loose charcoal in the bilge, blocking the flow of water to the pump. How did the water get into the ship? One of the crew simply left the porthole by his bunk open! Each time the ship plunged into a big wave, the porthole allowed water to come in. He was very sorry for his mistake and paid for it by having to sleep on a wet mattress for a day or so, which seemed a small punishment.

To show how things can happen fast, a year or so ago two West Indian crewmen were delivering a 40-foot sloop from Grenada to St. Lucia. Ten miles west of St. Vincent the boat split in half from stem to stern! This was not due to faulty workmanship at the factory, but to something that had been done to the sloop weeks before. In a marina, under the supervision of so-called professionals, a new stern gland had been forced into the old opening with a hydraulic jack. This gland acts as a bearing for the propeller shaft as it passes through the hull. Most fiberglass vessels are constructed in two halves, then the halves are glued together. Well, it's easy to see how the immense pressure of jacking the gland through the hull was just too much for the glue. It finally let go! Those two men were adrift in a small rubber dinghy for twelve days before a passing freighter picked them up.

But I had learned long ago not to dwell on possible mishaps; my thoughts were on the ship's work. I set the compass course and told Sidney that we should see the loom from Point Saline lighthouse on the south coast of Grenada at about midnight. I asked him who was on watch next, and what time.

"Ugh, what?" Sidney asked, dumbfounded, not understanding sea-going drill.

"Do you know what I'm talking about?" I asked.

"Captain, we never used the compass or stood watches before," he informed me.

Sidney was at the wheel, obviously very nervous. The others were standing in the back of the wheelhouse. I asked, "What's wrong with you guys?"

"We're scared, Captain, scared shitless."

"Okay," I said. "All of you go below and get something to eat and rest. I'll steer till midnight. Then I want Sidney to come up and steer for two hours, then Robbie for two hours. I'll be with you."

It was my job to teach these men to be seamen, and I had to start then. I put on a big front, showing no nervousness or fear, hoping to ease their tension. I hoped they all figured if I was fool enough to stay up there in the wheelhouse by myself, everything would be all right.

"Does that mean me too, Cap?" George asked.

"George, you know the engineer doesn't take a watch. You just check your engine room regularly."

Malcolm had guaranteed me that the ship would cruise at six or seven knots, which would mean about twelve hours traveling time from Trinidad to Grenada. Still, it took us eighteen hours before we had Point Saline's lighthouse on our beam. Obviously the bottom of the vessel was still very dirty. Our speed was only 4.8 knots. I was beginning to distrust Malcolm's word.

Arsenic poison is mixed with house paint and applied to the bottom of vessels to keep the marine animals from attaching themselves. This works for a while until the poison loses its strength, then the whole process is repeated. In the tropics, it's best to scrape and paint twice a year. But most people haul out their boats only once a year.

A few years back, my little watchdog Portnoy, a jet black Belgian schipperke, was killed playing around the docks where crewmen were painting the bottom of an island schooner. A sailor flicked paint onto the dog and he was dead before we could stop him from licking himself in an effort to clean his back.

Slogging along at 4.8 knots wasn't too bad on a beautiful day, especially in this part of the world. Over to starboard were the world famous Grenadines, a string of small islands, some populated, but most just barren rocks. It was a bright, sunny day, hot as usual. I was looking out across the deep blue waters toward these islands, dozens of them. I could see the fine ribbon of white sands on empty beaches, where driftwood from Lord knows where is left to bleach gray-white in the neverending sun. There were no man-made footprints on these beaches. No human spoils, no debris.

I thought of a line I'd read somewhere, "Rain to quench my thirst I need; an island in the stream, in the sun and wind alone." It reminded me of a time we were anchored in Admiralty Bay, Bequia, when suddenly one of the crew exclaimed, "Look, there's a school of robins!"

At the time I didn't know what a sea robin was. Soon we had robins, small, brownish-black fish, all around the boat and the crew were frantically getting their fishing tackle together. The line was the finest of thread and the hook was a small bent copper nail. That's right, bend a nail and shine it up. As soon as the nail touched the water, a fish would strike. A robin is similar to a herring in size and color, and excellent to eat. We were catching one for the pan and one for the bucket.

"What are we going to do with the ones in the bucket?" I asked.

"Cap, we gonna catch some big ones tonight," was the answer.

They changed the water in the bucket every so often, and the bait stayed alive for hours. We fished most of the night, and the next day the boys took ashore enough barracuda, skipjacks and other assorted fish, which we caught using the robins as bait, to buy food for a week.

The moral of this story is that in the tropics with nothing more than a shiny bent copper nail, you can eat; with a little tenacity, you are a trader.

Now Prune Island was coming into view. In an effort to sound more attractive to the tourists who visit its new hotel, it is now called Palm Island. And to my right was Mustique, where some wealthy developers were building secluded luxurious cottages. The developers had already built a small dirt airstrip there, which was locally known as one "helluva landing". The pilot had to come in over a hill before he could set down. In a loaded plane, the pilot had to skim that hill so close a passenger could count the piss-ants crawling around on the ground.

We were now passing the small island of Bequia, looking straight into Admiralty Bay, the finest natural harbor in the West Indies. I could see the town of Port Elizabeth, nestled around the end of the bay. This natural inlet could easily give shelter to a large part of the U.S. Navy Atlantic fleet. In the days of the French and English wars, it had been a most important base of naval operations.

"Sidney, I've decided we have to stop and clean the rest of the stuff off the bottom. Just head her toward Kingstown," I said.

It was obvious the crewmen were beginning to feel more comfortable. I'd be lying to say I hadn't worried about these men fitting into a shipboard routine. But not only were they fitting in, they were learning fast. Out of the five crewmembers, four were standing two-hour watches. And except for an occasional nap, I'd been right there on the bridge with them. I knew from experience that two hours at the wheel and six off gets old fast. No sooner do you fall asleep than some jerk is saying, "Get up! You're on watch," and you have to go back to work.

Pimp was becoming a problem. He was sullen and hated to take orders. The crew was hard on him, saying, "Hey, Pimp, what's your problem? You don't know your daddy?" Baldhead said, "Hell, it could be me. No, not so." Pimp grew more sullen.

"You son-of-a-bitch, you should talk. Do you even know your momma? I do," Pimp snarled. Everybody laughed. Pimp's face became contorted and showed genuine hate for the others.

A word they used endlessly was man, pronounced mon. I could never get used to that, it was so monotonous. They kidded each other, made jokes, and talked trash (a lot dirtier amongst themselves than in front of me). What women in the neighborhood was the best lay, who had the biggest or smallest cock. Always something to do with sex. This kind of rappin' went on day and night. It was their way of passing the time between watches when not asleep.

I said to myself, okay, let's keep things just like they are. This trip will be a piece of cake.

Soon, I could see Kingstown, St. Vincent. I hoped we could tie up alongside the jetty. To have the bottom cleaned, I really needed to be alongside. I could see an island schooner backing away. We were in luck.

"Sidney, take her in on the port side," I said.

"Aye, aye, sir," he answered, saluting, having fun. His round face crinkled into a smile.

"Don't be a smart ass."

Both of us were smiling. We were surrounded by little boys, swimming out, asking for coins to be tossed into the water. This made a wonderful picture. Here were these little brown faces beaming up at us, shouting, "Skip, throw me a quarter! Look, Skip, look at me! Hey, look at me!" Multiply that by fifteen or twenty, and you have quite a lot of noise. Their naked bodies glistened just below the surface, and the sun sparkling off the white water kicked up by their feet was something to see. I had a few coins, and I tossed one out in the middle of the bunch. Suddenly five or six little bodies would dive down to grab the coin, as much as twenty feet deep. In the optic-clear water I could see the coin at that depth easily. Each time the coin turned over and over going down, the sun would reflect off its surface and flash a beam of light up. Soon the beam became weaker, till it disappeared.

These kids made good money when the cruise ships visited the island. Most cruise ships anchored out in the bay and used their lifeboats to ferry passengers back and forth to shore. The little boys would paddle a boat or a homemade raft out to the ship, where they would beg for coins, U.S. preferred. Some of the boys would wait on shore and ask for coins there, but they never had as much luck as the divers. How did the divers keep the coins they retrieved while swimming? In their mouths, of course.

CHAPTER 5

"If I Could Get Away, I Would Go with You"

At one time, St. Vincent had achieved a degree of prosperity. Copra (coconut) was flourishing, arrowroot was very popular for thickening gravy, and the bananas were doing just fine. Tourism also brought in a few bucks. The future looked hopeful.

Then came the decline of the copra and the arrowroot. Coconut oil was deemed unhealthy, and arrowroot was replaced with less expensive ingredients. Now the only export was bananas. Each week the banana boat arrived and, day or night, the local bananas were ready to go on board. The boat made a weekly circuit (actually two boats alternated) through the islands to pick up the fruit and get it back to England before it began to ripen. It was critical not to waste time anywhere. If the vessel or the schedule broke down, even for a day, the whole shipload of bananas could become overripe before they reached the market.

Finally we docked in Kingstown around four o'clock, having been at sea for nearly two days and only traveling 190 miles. It was quite disappointing. After finishing with Customs and Immigration, I went ashore and called Malcolm in Trinidad.

"Malcolm, we're in Kingstown, St. Vincent. Our speed is down to 4.8 knots. Some struts in the bow section are loose. We need to finish cleaning the bottom, and Robbie has to do some welding in the bow," I said.

"Hire some divers and I'll see you tomorrow," Malcolm said, his tone of voice indicating nothing. Was this guy made of ice? Did he have any feelings?

"Okay, bye," I said. I wasn't mad yet, but I was starting to worry. He had not kept his word on the hull cleaning or the injectors.

I spread the word around the dock that I needed divers, and in five minutes I had more than enough. Eight or ten young fellows were soon diving to beat the band with their brand new putty knives. The water in the harbor was very clear, and the boys were doing a great job. Most kids in the West Indies learn to swim and dive early in life. Their mothers take them down for a daily swim and a bath in the sea. On the small islands, this is how most of the people bathe.

Malcolm appeared around ten the next morning, looking very dapper in his travelling suit and tie. After he changed clothes, he and Robbie disappeared into the bow section. They spent ten or fifteen minutes down in the bow examining the damage. When they finally climbed out, very hot and sweaty, Robbie went to work gathering his welding equipment.

Robbie had his work cut out for him. Ten or fifteen horizontal struts (the steel channels which run fore and aft between the hulls ribs) were broken and needed to be welded back in place. Being the youngest on board and an East Indian, too, he got a lot of kidding, but Robbie was an expert welder and was learning to be a fine ship engineer under George's tutoring. Of course we did not allow him to work alone; there was always someone watching him, looking out for the possible build-up of carbon monoxide gas. There was no way to extract these gases, so about every twenty or thirty minutes, Robbie would come out of the bow to get some fresh air.

I took this time out to visit some of my drinking buddies up at the Mariners Inn. I sat down with Dave, the owner and manager, a Canadian who had been down in the islands for five or six years, and we gossiped for two or three hours. We discussed the ship and the mission I was on. Dave agreed that I was a damn fool, "But if I could get away, I'd go with you," he said with sincerity.

Dave and I had done a lot of sailing together. One night, a couple of years earlier, we were going down to Grenada to participate in the annual sports fishing tournament. I was renting a beach house called the Pink Cottage. Dave's 40-foot sloop was anchored out from the beach. We were supposed to leave St. Vincent at ten o'clock at night from the lagoon, just above Young Island, but it was eleven before we got on board and underway. My dog Bo, an eleven-month-old South African ridgeback, had swum out, wanting to go along, but I yelled for him to go back ashore. It was so dark I couldn't see him, but I could hear him splashing after us. We sailed through the reef and out into the open channel, with him back there trying to keep up. If there had been any way I could have seen him in the dark, choppy water, I would have gone back and picked him up. It was excruciating to leave him in the dark alone, swimming for his life, two hundred yards from shore. At the time I told Dave I wasn't worried. I said Bo could swim all the way to Grenada if he had to. We continued on through the night and arrived the next day at St. Georges. I was so upset, I hitched a ride right back to St. Vincent on a friend's schooner. Bo had made it back fine.

Malcolm Coma had changed. In Trinidad, I had seen him joke with the crew, and he was amiable with me, but since his arrival in St. Vincent, he'd been aloof, distant, unfriendly. He did not joke with the crew or offer to have lunch with me ashore. It took me a while to figure it out. He was worried. Worried about us? Hell, no! He was worried about his ship and the cargo we were going to deliver . . . about us making it! If we got to the Dominican Republic and loaded the equipment there and delivered it to Guadeloupe, he would receive $20,000 for the trip, but we were already costing him some of that loot.

I felt I knew what I was doing in this situation, but Malcolm didn't. He'd sent five West Indians and me, out on this old boat, hoping we would make it. It's like sending someone across a thinly frozen pond and saying, "You go ahead, I'm sure the ice will hold you." He'd let money cloud his judgment, or maybe he had none to begin with.

Not bothering to say goodbye, Malcolm flew back to Trinidad on the island hopper the next day, and we kept on working. It took another two days to complete the welding and scraping the bottom. We'd been out five days from San Fernando and traveled only 190 miles!

Now, the trip was becoming a challenge. We were going to make it to the Dominican Republic, regardless.

Charles, a Vincentian I'd met while partying at the Mariners Inn, came on board and we killed some time drinking beer. His job was with the tourist board and he asked if I'd like to go on a picnic the next day. He was taking some Americans on a climb up Soufrière, an extinct volcano.

"I sure could use the company," was what he said, but he really was worried someone might need help making it to the top or back down.

"Well, I wish I could think of a good excuse not to go, but what the hell!"

The volcano is located at the north end of the island, and it takes quite a while to get there, so we left early the next morning by car, driving up the paved road along the east side or Atlantic side of the island. St. Vincent's beaches are black, a result of volcano lava being ground up into fine particles. White sand beaches are the result of ancient coral reefs being ground up the same way. This side of the island was called Windward, and had a great deal of flat land for growing arrowroot, vegetables, copra and, of course, bananas.

Charles and I started climbing with our four tourists around ten o'clock, first through a huge copra plantation, with its row upon row of coconut palms. You should never stand under one of these palms; those nuts falling can crush your own nut real easy. Next we were into thick jungle, climbing over dead tree trunks and up steep hills. This was hard going for me, and the tourists were not hardy. They were not used to the constant climbing, and were sweating from the intense tropical heat, so I know they suffered badly. The volcano is 1,233 feet high, which doesn't sound like much, but the physical effort to reach the top is considerable. One fellow, in his fifties, was bringing up the rear and had fallen way behind. After about an hour, we broke into the clear. No more vegetation—from then on, just loose lava gravel. In some places I would take two steps forward and slip back one.

The tropical sun was climbing towards it summit. I had my doubts about the guy in the rear. Our guide, Charles, dropped back to check on him, but the man waved him on, saying he was all right. From the base of the mountain to the rim of the volcano, it took us two and a half-hours. No one even bothered to look over into the abyss at first; we just flopped down, exhausted. Charles, who'd been there several times, saved the day by passing around a small bottle of Jackiron, the local rum. One swig and we were on our feet and ready to go.

We edged over to the precipice and looked down. Five or six hundred feet below was a light blue opaque lake about a quarter of a mile in diameter. The inside walls of the volcano were almost vertical, so we felt safer lying down to view the scene. To the west we could see for limitless miles, but there were clouds all around us otherwise. The guy who'd fallen behind never did make it to the top. We found him totally exhausted lying by the trail on our way back, what a waste of energy. Five years back, a man had a heart attack climbing up Soufrière.

Back at the boat, Michael, one of the Vincentian divers, impressed me. He was young, about twenty, clean cut and articulate. He pleaded for me to take him on the voyage, saying there was no future for him on St. Vincent and no way for him to get a decent job. We needed another deck hand: I hired him. Michael claimed to be the nephew of the ex-premier, Clarence Blade. Mr. Blade was not an honest man; I should have had doubts about his nephew.

The young fellows were nearly finished scraping the bottom, so I decided to check myself. I had no swimsuit, but there were no women on the dock, so I took off my shorts and dove in with only my jockeys on. I found the only areas the boys needed to touch up were along the keel, the hardest part naturally.

When I finally climbed back on board, soaking wet, I looked up and right there on the dock was an automobile and, standing beside the machine, of course, was a woman. She happened to be a friend of mine, Betsy, a lovely young lady from Rhode Island. Betsy had come down to the islands to enjoy paradise and was now the assistant manager at one of the island hotels down in the Grenadines, Petit St. Vincent. She insisted we go for a drink at the Mariners Inn. I quickly changed my drawers, put on some decent clothes, and we were off. Betsy came up to St. Vincent two or three times a month. She would do her shopping and catch the mail boat back down the islands the next morning. If you don't have a home to go to or a boat, there's little else to do but go to some bar, sit around and nurse a drink. So we sat around reminiscing, gossiping and just enjoying catching up.

The bar at the Mariners Inn was kind of different. It was a twenty-foot flying fish boat sunk into the ground out on the patio. Occasionally one of the flying fish boats operating out of Barbados, which is directly upwind from St. Vincent, breaks down and the engine won't start. So they drift for a couple of days, ending up on the beach here. If by chance they miss St. Vincent, the next stop is maybe Aruba or Curaçao, about two hundred miles away, if they make it at all. The poor fishermen who own the boats have to sell them because they are unable to motor up against the trade winds and make it back home.

By the time Betsy drove me back to the dock, the boys had finished the cleaning and repairs and we were ready to go to sea again.

CHAPTER 6

Black Power Mutiny

On December 15, at about three o'clock in the afternoon, we backed away from the dock and I set a course for the northwestern tip of Puerto Rico. My landfall would be the Cabo Rojo lighthouse. I expected to pick up the loom from many miles away at sea. This would be the longest open sea voyage we would make without seeing land. I hoped everything and everyone would hang together!

Sidney, Baldhead, Robbie and Pimp had taken an interest in learning about the compass and a little navigation, and had picked up the steering quickly, but Michael, the new man, couldn't seem to keep his mind on the work. Every time I checked the compass, he would be off course by five or ten degrees.

"Michael," I said, "if you don't pay attention to the compass course, we'll never find Puerto Rico."

His reply was always an indifferent shrug of his shoulders or he would suck between his teeth. Michael, who was black and about twenty-three or twenty-four, had light skin and a good build, not muscular, but strong anyway. I hoped he would break out of his funk; still, his attitude bothered me. I didn't want to start raising hell, not yet. But, after a couple of days of constant badgering, I finally blew up. I'd gone down below to relieve myself, and when I came back on the bridge, Michael was a full fifteen degrees off course.

"Look at your compass—you're fifteen degrees off course! What the hell is the matter with you?" I shouted.

"Cap, I can't do this job. Is there somethin' else I can do?" he asked, looking down at his bare feet at the same time. I knew he could do the work. He was lying.

"Get this in your head one time," I replied. "Your job is to help steer this damn boat. You gonna do your job or not? If you think you can get out of doing your watch, you're more stupid than I thought." I was furious, and he knew it.

My cabin was back of the wheelhouse; therefore, I had no reason to move around the ship very much. Baldhead would bring me something to eat when I asked him, so I had no idea what was going on down in the crew's cabin. I had my first inkling that something was wrong when Baldhead came on watch, obviously very mad. He was standing at the wheel shirtless, sweating, muttering and cussing to himself. He looked like he would explode.

"What's bothering you?" I asked, looking at this big man.

"Nothin' for you to fret about, Captain," Baldhead answered.

I soon forgot about the incident because just then the port engine stopped. I told Baldhead to compensate with the wheel and to get us back on course. I ran down to the engine room hatch and slid down the ladder. George was standing by the port engine scratching his head. He was dressed in an old pair of tattered shorts, made out of worn-out long pants, no shirt or shoes. The noise from the starboard engine, the diesel generator, the pumps and electric motors was deafening.

George shouted, "Cap, don't ask me why. I don't know yet. Give me a few minutes to figure this out."

I went back up on deck and looked around. The sky was clear, the sea was calm, birds flying to their next chance meal; it was a beautiful day. We were going around in a big circle. I ran up to the bridge.

"Baldhead, what the hell are you doing?" I asked.

"Captain, this is it. She's hard to starboard," Baldhead said.

I thought, damn, she will not steer on one engine. If we couldn't get that engine going, we were in serious trouble.

Normally a twin-engine vessel will steer quite well on one engine, but this one was different. It took me a while, but I figured it out. The engines were spaced too far apart. The propeller acted like an oar pushing the ship to the left, and the rudder behind the prop wasn't large enough to compensate. I told Baldhead to idle back the starboard engine and we would wait. We were sitting in the middle of the Caribbean Sea with no place to go except in circles.

As we waited for George to get the machine running again, a thought edged into my mind. If the engine had internal damage, which we could not fix in the ocean, we were virtually helpless.

In most situations, a man feels he can cope with any circumstance he might encounter. One way or another, the problem can be solved, maybe not to everyone's satisfaction, but something can be done. It would be extremely difficult to imagine a case where a solution couldn't be found. But here we were in the middle of the ocean, not knowing whether we would have to float for endless days hoping to be spotted by a passing freighter, or drift till we finally went aground on some unknown shore.

"Lordy mercy," Baldhead muttered, looking at me with a helpless gesture of his hands.

This situation reminded me of a dismal night a few years back. I was approaching the harbor at Gibraltar when both my engines stopped. I knew why. I'd

inadvertently emptied the main fuel tanks without
changing over to the spare ones. At the time, I felt it
would be prudent to ask for help, damn fast. The protec-
tive stone breakwater, which guards the harbor walls,
was only two hundred yards away, and the wind was
blowing me toward the rocks. I got on the radio and
called the harbor police, asking them to come out and
give me a hand.

"Jolly good, old chap, we'll be out shortly," was the
reply. In the meantime I went down into the engine room
and switched over the tanks. The reason I was worried
was simple. If the fuel pumps sucked air into the system,
I'd be on the rocks before I could bleed the air from the
lines. The next question: would the engines start, would
the police arrive in time, or would the rocks claim another unhappy traveler? The engines started without any
hesitation. I went into the old submarine pens (used during World War II) where all foreign arriving yachts are
supposed to go, and waited for the police launch. In
about thirty minutes they arrived.

"You look frustrated. What happened?" I asked the
sergeant.

"Well, sir, we were on our way out to give emergency assistance to this bloke what was drifting onto the
outer wall, when one of our other launches ran straight
into a mooring buoy. One of the big ones we use for battleships and such. The launch sank straight away, and we
diverted our attention to the rescue of them blokes," the
police sergeant said.

"What happened to the yacht in distress?" I asked.

"Well, now, that's a good question. Marty, ask cen-
tral if that yacht is okay," he said.

"Don't bother," I said. "I'm the bloke on the yacht!"

There wasn't much of anything we could do now
but cool our heels. We waited about an hour before we

heard the engine start up and come to life. That was close, I thought. The sun was bearing down on us, because standing still like that heats up a steel ship something awful, and by the time we got underway again, I was soaked with sweat.

When George finally came on the bridge, I asked, "What the hell happened back there?"

He took his time answering. Just about the time I was going to ask him again, he spoke.

"Cap, we ran her too long. She needed to rest and cool off."

"George, watch those machines real close," I said. "This old tub won't steer on one engine. We've been going around in a circle."

"I could've told you that, Cap," George said. "A couple years ago we were towed in from off Moruga on the south coast. The port engine quit again, and we was driftin' out into the ocean. See how dark Sidney is? Well, that day he was white as a ghost. All of us was scared, the Orinoco river kicks a ship out to sea down there. We had another little guy, short and fat, named Buddy. He got so nervous, he started to bawl. Finally I smacked him hard. I figured he might as well have somethin' to cry about."

"Well, what happened?" I asked, anxious to know the ending.

"Just about dark, from out of nowhere came the entire Japanese shrimp boat fleet. They fish south of here around the mouth of the Amazon and Orinoco rivers. Like I said, it was gettin' dark, so we had to make a signal. The only thing we could do was set somethin' on fire. We set a whole bunch of oily rags from the engine room on fire. We was jumpin' up and down, shoutin' for help; not lookin' at what was happenin', and by accident, we set the ship on fire," George said.

"You did what?" I asked in disbelief.

"We set the ship on fire. It was an accident . . . but

there we were, jumpin' around while the ship burned. When your life is on the line, Cap, you don't give a damn about no damn rust bucket," was his reply.

"Did the Japanese come over and rescue you?" I asked.

"Yeah, one boat in each fleet is fixed with a heavy duty pump for just that reason, to put out fires and stuff. Them guys were real quick. It didn't take them five minutes to hose us down. We was hooked up and they was towin' us in no time at all. Saved our asses for sure," George said.

"Did you thank them?" I asked.

"We sure did," Sidney cut in. "If it hadn't been for them we'd have starved pretty quick or burned, 'cause all we had on board was three or four pounds of rice, that was our emergency supplies. You know what they did? They gave us two boxes of bar shrimp (about ten pounds)."

"What's bar shrimp?" I asked.

"That's the best. If you ever get a chance to eat some, you'll know what I'm taking about. They're pinky-white, 'bout twenty to the pound and no vein (don't ask me why, maybe they'd just been to the john). The Japanese have a man to sort through and pick out the best. The fleet was headed for the shipyard at Chagaramas. They used the bar shrimp to bribe the dock master. That and some money will get them hauled out and the bottom of the boats painted real quickly," George said.

The crew, except for Pimp and Michael, were all inside the wheelhouse. I was the captain, the odd man out. I hoped these men didn't detest me too much, for this was going to be a long journey.

Suddenly, the wheelhouse was full of the sound of drumsticks chattering away. Someone was using the steel roof as a drum, and it was deafening. We rushed out onto the starboard wing, and there they were, Pimp and Michael, playing the fools, but looking proud and defiant.

I shouted, "Get your ass down from there. What the hell do you think you're doing? This is a damn ship, not a playpen." I was frustrated and mad as hell. After they slowly climbed down, I said, "Pull a stunt like that again and we'll have a very serious situation on our hands, get my drift?"

Was this a childish prank or what? I couldn't figure out what was happening with these two men, so the next time Baldhead came on watch, I said, "Baldhead, what the hell is going on? Now you best tell me before this goes too far!"

"Captain, Michael is preachin' *black power*," Baldhead said, looking down at the deck.

"What the hell does that mean?"

"Well, I can tell you one thing. He wants you dead," Baldhead said.

"Are you serious—he's going to try to kill me?"

"Captain, he's talkin' about us takin' the ship. It don't make no sense to us, but he's crazy, and won't shut up," Baldhead said.

"Who's with me and who's not?" I asked with concern.

"Don't you fret none, Cap, it's just Michael and Pimp. We won't let it go no further," Baldhead said.

I should have known Pimp would be in on it. I'd heard a little about this black power movement which had spread from the States down to the Caribbean. The self-appointed leaders were preaching revolution against anyone in authority, including local governments, police, churches and schools. Some islands had gangs of these Black Panthers. All over the Caribbean the police were having a difficult time coping. Now it looked like it was my turn.

Michael had no trouble converting Pimp; you might say Pimp had an empty head, and anything exciting appealed to him. Where Robbie was slight, Pimp was angular, with long arms, and a long neck. He reminded me of a black Ichabod Crane. He thrived on being against the majority. But thank goodness that wasn't the case with the others. Baldhead told me of arguing with Michael for hours and not getting anywhere.

"Michael can't read, so he persuades Pimp to read to him," Sidney said. "He's tryin' to memorize what the papers say. They hide 'em in the old heater we don't use. Baldhead says he's gonna burn 'em the first chance he gets."

We learned later that Michael had been brainwashed by his next door neighbor back in St. Vincent, and believed he was a true Black Muslim.

Michael apparently felt he was part of the Muslim movement that came into existence in the late sixties, after the prison riots at Attica and Rahway. Men like Malcolm X, Huey P. Newton, Eldridge Cleaver and Bobby Seale declared, "Arm or be harmed. It's better to die as men fighting racism than to live under oppression." The Black Muslim philosophy was in direct conflict with the teachings of Martin Luther King. King, a preacher, and the Panther leaders, mostly convicted felons, presented quite a choice for the black community, one advocating the violent overthrow of authority by force and the other proclaiming, "We shall overcome," by peaceful means.

Baldhead told me Michael had lived next door to a man who was deported from the States because of his involvement with the Black Panthers. This man was highly motivated and preached his philosophy to anyone who would listen. Michael became a disciple and was constantly in trouble with the St. Vincent police. When we docked in Kingstown, Michael had seen a way to get out from under his so-called oppressors. But we became his new target.

Some of the former British islands, now independent, had elected black government officials, black police, black school teachers and black church leaders (the Catholic Church alone had maintained white clergy), and everyone else in authority was black as well. It made no sense to me why black power would become important down here in the West Indies. Within a very few months, virtually all the West Indies would have independence.

"Sidney, why is Michael preaching this revolt stuff?" I asked. "You people already have the power."

"In the States the black man is fighting the whites for equality, buckin' the establishment. Down here in the islands, the Panthers buck the black establishment. They say the blacks in power control the wealth, and the rest of the people have nothing now and won't ever have anything. We think maybe it's true, but we don't believe we'd be any better off with these crazy asses runnin' things either," Sidney said.

I was amazed. Sidney's clear and concise explanation surprised me.

"What's the solution—communism?" I inquired.

"All Michael will say is that we have to get rid of anyone in authority," Sidney said. "He'd better watch out though. Baldhead and the rest of us are really mad. He won't let up; day and night, the same old stuff. Robbie asked him the other day, 'What'd you do if you did get rid of the skipper?' Michael said, 'We'd just go home!'"

"'That's the dumbest thing you ever said,' Robbie told him. 'Look outside! Do you see land? You dumb bastard, you couldn't get us home. You can't navigate . . . hell, you can't even read!'

"Then Michael came back with, 'The black man is smart; he's the smartest on earth. Didn't man come from Ethiopia in the beginnin'? We started it all! Why should we be slaves to the wealthy blacks and the whites? Join up and help us take back what's ours.'"

The next time Michael came on watch, I asked him, "What's all this talk about you wanting the crew to take over the vessel?"

"Captain, we's just arguing politics. It ain't got nothin' to do with you," Michael said. "Don't let them others poison your mind against me." There was a half smile on his lips. His whole arrogant behavior convinced me he was lying through his teeth.

Still, his answer was rather smooth, I thought.

"Well, let me tell you something, Michael," I said. "Do you have any idea how long you would go to jail for mutiny? You'd be an old man before you got out. I guarantee that. So cool off on that political gibberish before you get into serious trouble, understand?"

Later that night Baldhead told Michael that they'd had enough of his shit and didn't want to hear any more talk about taking over the vessel.

Michael's comeback was, "See there, that's what I'm talkin' about. You're just a slave to that white man."

"Damn you, shut up," Baldhead had yelled.

After this blowup, things seemed to quiet down, and we went about the business of getting to the Dominican Republic. The weather was good. The dreaded *Christmas winds* (the beginning of the winter trade winds) looked like they were going to hold off for a while.

In the tropics there are two main seasons. The hurricane season begins at the spring equinox, with variable winds, rain and of course the occasional hurricane. The other season begins with the autumn equinox, with light winds during November and part of December. Around Christmas-time the northeast trade winds start to blow, usually twenty to thirty knots for a week or two, then slowing down to a gentler fifteen to twenty knots. This is the perfect time to sail these waters which, of course, is why it is the tourist season.

George and Robbie were fishing off the stern, hors-
ing around, trying to push each other into the sea off the
stern of the boat. West Indians always fish when underway. They were doing quite well, catching dolphin fish
and skipjack, when suddenly a large triangular fin appeared just behind the boat.

"Shark, shark!" shouted Robbie. "Run for your
lives!" and he ran up the deck in a flash. He scared everybody, but Robbie wasn't running from fear, he was
running to get his shark rig. His line was very heavy
nylon, a long steel leader with a big hook. Once back on
the stern he hooked a small mackerel up and threw it
right in front of the shark's nose. That old shark must
have been hungry, because he just opened his mouth
and swallowed the bait. Robbie took a turn around a
bollard and was paying out line. Suddenly realizing he
was hooked, the fish jumped up in the air and shook
his head to the left and to the right, arching his body
into a near perfect circle. He threw spray forty feet in
either direction and pulled as hard as he could, but
could not break the bond and rid himself of the awful
pain in his stomach. As hard as that fish tried, he could
not regain his freedom. He dove down to a depth of a
hundred feet, and then the line tightened and he fought
it again, with no luck. After ten minutes or so, he
turned and swam as hard as he could toward the surface, breaking out into the open air. His whole body
came clear of the water, twisting back and forth, back
and forth, trying to free himself of this damnable pain
in his guts. He fell back into the sea exhausted, trying
to get his breath, having been unable to breathe while
he was fighting.

"George, give me a hand!" Robbie shouted. "I can't
haul him in by myself."

"Okay, but if he runs, I'm throwin' down."

"Come on, old man, can't you taste them steaks?

Where's Baldhead? We need help with this monster," Robbie said.

"I'm comin', I'm comin', don't loose it. You're shark bait if you do."

The three of them hauled the shark up onto the stern of the ship. It was a white-tip about eight feet long. The boys killed the shark with several blows across the head with a piece of two-inch pipe. Baldhead cut a fillet off one side; it must have weighed twenty pounds. They left the rest lying on the aft deck. When I asked why, Robbie replied, "Just to look at it for a while, then we'll throw it overboard."

Someone had opened the mouth and stuck a stick in to hold it open. God, those teeth looked vicious. They were fairly easy to remove, so I got a couple as souvenirs.

CHAPTER 7

A Banana Republic

We'd been at sea for four and a half days, and late in the afternoon, we finally saw land. I knew, more or less, where we were, hopefully off the northwest coast of Puerto Rico. We changed course to port (I always steer a little to starboard of any landfall, so if I miss finding it, I know which way to turn) and ran along the coast till finally I identified the Cabo Rojo lighthouse. When the light flashed, we could see the outline of the tall, slender structure, painted white as usual. Few people know or understand what it means to find an aid to navigation like this after being out at sea for days, maybe weeks.

I knew exactly where we were now, about to enter the Mona Passage. The moon was three-quarters full, so there was a chance we could have a decent crossing tonight. The Mona is famous for being rough on sailors and ships. Because of its rip tides, creating a confused sea with large, lumpy waves coming from every direction, it can be very dangerous, especially to smaller boats. The night was dark, the wind was a breeze, and there was a gentle swell coming in from the northeast. The trade winds hadn't begun yet. We picked up the loom of the Isla Saona lighthouse on the Dominican Republic southeast coast just before dawn, and we steered a course to stay clear of the dangerous set of reefs that extend off the southeast coast.

Daylight found us off the southern tip of the island,

and now we could head in toward Santo Domingo. Once I had a good fix, we ran up the coast and finally I located the Bay of Azua.

"This is it," I said, pleased at our successful trip.

Our destination was the port of Azua, a disused banana boat loading facility. Neither the dock nor the storage shed had been utilized for the shipment of bananas since the blight destroyed the whole crop a few years ago.

Trujillo, the infamous dictator, had been getting rich off the bananas until the blight came and ruined everything. The people also had began to enjoy a better life, and when the bananas were finished, the people turned on Trujillo, killing him and his mistress.

A few years back, I was visiting the island and asked a taxi driver, "Did you see Trujillo killed?"

"Si, Señor, I was there and I got a little piece of him," he said.

"What'd you do with it? I asked.

"I ate it," he said with a big grin. "We all ate a piece of him till he was all gone."

"That's hard to believe. What about the bones?" I asked.

"Some people took a few. The dogs took the rest," he laughed.

"You will never find his grave; there isn't any," he continued. "You saw pictures of him in the newspaper hanging upside down naked. Well, after that we eat him. We allow no more pictures. Señor, we were thousands and thousands, and he was one man with all the money, more money than is possible to spend, and we had nothing. Now some of us own land. We farm, we are our own boss. Just like you."

I had to check this story out, and later, I found it was true from talking to other witnesses.

Our mission was to transport an entire oil well
drilling outfit from Azua to Basse-Terre, Guadeloupe. I
looked into the bay for a dock or shed, a sign of the oil
well drilling outfit, anything. It was a fine looking bay,
but empty.

"Take her in and drop the anchor," I said. "We'll get
a good night's sleep and find the right bay tomorrow."

I climbed down to the main deck, and everybody
was walking around, relaxing. Robbie was talking to
George, trying to explain about the cactus which they
had never seen before, when suddenly we heard machine gun fire, and the unmistakable whine of bullets
passing overhead. We all ducked down behind the three-
foot steel bulwarks that run along the sides of the main
deck. I peeked over the top to see what was going on. An
army officer was frantically waving his arms, and men in
uniforms, soldiers, were running in every direction, taking up defensive positions. I thought, hell these guys
have real guns!

I peeked over once more and the officer started
jumping up and down, waving his arms and shouting.
I thought, he's waving at us! I stood up and waved
back. Another ten minutes went by, then I could see
them launching a row boat. Two officers (always
standing) and a man at the oars were heading our
way. It wouldn't be long now till we knew what was
happening.

The officer, who seemed to be in charge, introduced
himself. He seemed nervous but was smiling. A good
sign.

"I am Major José Morales, Dominican Republic
Army. I am the commandant of the garrison at the port of
Azua. Who are you who have trespassed on our territo-
rial waters?" he asked in Spanish. He was a dandy, right
out of a comic opera. A little fat man with a waxed mus-

tache, which he twirled around between his fingers continuously, he wore an immaculate uniform, with Sam Brown belt and pistol holster.

In English, I replied, "I'm real glad to meet you. I am Captain Bob Hudson. We are from Trinidad and we look for the port of Azua. And is this indeed that port?"

"No, no, no, you have made a big mistake. The port is three kilometers down the coast. Are you here about the oil drilling equipment?"

"Yes, we are," I replied.

"Would you like for me to guide you?" asked the commandant.

His knowledge of the English language was remarkable.

"I would be honored, Commandant," I said. The other officer was Navy. He was tall and aloof, and had little to say. His uniform was not as well kept as the major's.

I asked, "How many men do you have in your command, sir?"

"Fifteen men and one officer," he replied without hesitation.

I found it interesting that both the Navy and the Army were required to guard this facility. I asked again, "*Comandante*, how many men do you have under your command?"

"Ah, my new friend, you know too much about our business already."

I would say he was in his late forties and very excitable. He told me over coffee the next day, "I really thought you were Cubans and that I would be killed."

"My dear new friend, we were the ones frightened. Your bullets were like harbingers from hell. I'll tell you the truth; at that moment I was thinking, if they fire a bazooka, we're all dead. From your actions onshore, I expected no less."

"Capitán, I must apologize for that mistake. My overzealous gunnery sergeant's weapon went off by accident. You will be happy to know I slap him upside his stupid head," and the Major giggled.

The commandant was beginning to relax and was obviously enjoying himself. There was a twinkle in those dark eyes, and I would guess, given half a chance, he could be mischievous. He gave me a short history of the facility and the reasons why it was not used.

"Why, at one time this place was alive with workers in the storage shed and out on the docks. Women singing, each night there was fiesta. Capitán, I miss those days." He looked sad.

He talked of his beliefs about Azua's future and about his and his men's future.

"Just this morning in the Santo Domingo newspaper, our scientists announced they have discovered a cure for the banana blight. By this time next year we will be planting new crops of bananas and everything will be back like it was before," the *comandante* said, looking at me to see if I disagreed.

By now we were rounding a headland, and I could see into the bay. There was the dock and storage shed. "Sidney," I said, "take her in on the port side."

The shed was about two hundred feet long and half that wide; the dock and shed were in excellent condition, clean and well painted. Behind the shed, as far as I could see, was a huge open field where the bananas had once thrived. Now the field was completely covered with tomato vines, which were commercially grown for a company in the States. Twice a year the company would bring in mechanical pickers to harvest the ripe fruit, which was then loaded into a refrigerated ship and taken away. The local population would work for a couple of weeks, and then nothing.

The Army and Navy were garrisoned inside this shed. It seemed their primary duty was to guard the oil drilling equipment.

We docked and the commandant said he would call the Customs and Immigrations officials. He would also notify the agent for the Texas owners, or ex-owners, I should say, of the oil drilling rig.

It was nine o'clock that evening before they arrived, because the two men were forced to hitch a ride out to the port from Santo Domingo, some sixty miles away!

We in the United States take it for granted that government officials have vehicles to take them anywhere, anytime. This is not true for other parts of the world.

It was two in the morning before we were free to go to bed. I was very tired, having stayed up with each man at the wheel most of the time during the voyage. I told the men that tomorrow we would load the old tub and head back south. It was December 19, and we'd been out nine days from San Fernando. We hoped to be back by Christmas. I thought about my wife: was she doing okay, was she as horny as I was? Maybe I could call her tomorrow.

The next morning, I went to the back of the shed to have a look at the cargo we were going to transport. I was shocked. The equipment covered over an acre, drilling pipe, casement pipe, generators, motors, there was even a Mac truck with the pipe tower on it, and a small portable office building. It was quite obvious that we would have to make two trips. I thought to myself, did Malcolm know? The bastard!

I went back to the ship and broke the news to the crew. No one said a word for a few seconds, then everybody started talking at once. George said,

"I got children who believe in Santa Claus! I have to be home."

All I could say was, "I'm sorry. You can be sure that Mr. Coma will hear about this in no uncertain terms."

It is extremely difficult to describe how disappointment affects different individuals. George knew it was useless to protest. He was staring at the bulkhead. In his mind, I'm sure, he was visualizing his wife and family. He let out a sigh and muttered, "Shit." Sitting there shirtless on a piece of drilling equipment, he suddenly slammed his right fist into his left; every muscle in his chest and back tightened and flexed.

Sidney and Robbie, being East Indians, had different customs and religious holidays than the others. Even so, they would miss the spirit of the Christmas season. One thing is for sure; in the West Indies, everyone joins in and takes part in any sort of celebration, regardless. These people, on the whole, have very few material things, but they are a happy lot.

Baldhead was saying, "There's gonna be a lot of disappointed ladies around San Fernando this Christmas."

"Why?" I asked.

"Who's gonna give 'em what I usually gives 'em?" he said.

"Hell, maybe they'll get somethin' 'big' in their stockings this year!" George said with a wink, his face breaking open with a big smile.

"Captain, you see anything big about him?" Baldhead asked.

I shook my head. No way was I getting into this.

"What's big about me you don't see, Head."

In some of the islands in the West Indies, there is a strange custom that takes place each year around Christmas time. Twelve nights before Christmas, the young people (and some not so young) set out walking just after sundown, usually alone, but sometimes in pairs. As they meet the opposite sex on the road, regardless of whom it is (except their own kin), they exchange greetings, go off the road to a secluded spot and have intercourse. When they are finished, they get up, say thank you, goodbye, and start the whole process over again. This strange custom goes on every night for twelve nights! One Christmas we were waiting for a charter to start in St. Vincent. Our usual taxi driver, Calvin, who was in his early twenties, gave us a day by day account of his nightly wanderings. It was unbelievable! Twelve nights, all night long. Now this was supposed to be just for unmarried men and women. I understand that during this time, it's hard to find anyone who is married, or who will admit it.

While the oil drilling equipment was being loaded on the aft deck, we were all busy tying the stuff down to make sure it would stay put. I told Robbie to weld everything he could to other equipment and to the ship, making it solid. Deck cargo is extremely dangerous at any time; if it moves from side to side when the ship rolls, it could cause the vessel to capsize, and we were taking this equipment across the dreaded Mona Passage.

The Mona Passage is one of the main sources of water from the Atlantic into the Caribbean Sea. The other source is the Anegada Passage. Sure, water enters between the other islands, but not nearly enough. The Mona and the Anegada are wide, and they allow massive amounts of water to go in and out twice a day. When this mass of water goes back out into the Atlantic and meets the prevailing trade winds, a very confused sea with huge breaking waves coming from all directions is created. We call it "wind against tide," and it can get very exciting. The worst time for these conditions is during spring tides, which happen when the moon is either full or new. We have either spring tides or neap tides every change of the moon, or twice a month. A small boat should definitely stay away from these open channels when spring tides are ebbing.

Small yacht sailors, contemplating a cruise to the Caribbean islands, save themselves a lot of grief by keeping up with the moon and tides. Even though the rise and fall of the tide is quite small, the currents can be very strong in certain areas, especially at spring tides. Channel crossings should suit the tides, not convenience.

CHAPTER 8

Crossing the Anegada

On December 20, we left Azua for Basse-Terre. The weather was fine, sunny and warm and everything was going well until we left the lee. Then the full force of the trade winds, blowing half-a-gale, twenty to twenty-five knots, was coming in from the east. Mona would surely be rough on us tonight. The Christmas winds had arrived.

The oil drilling rig we were transporting belonged to a Texas company that had been wildcatting all over the Dominican Republic. They'd drilled five dry holes, each over a mile deep, and then gave up. The Texans sold the rig to some French speculators who hoped to strike hot water or steam on Guadeloupe. All the islands are volcanic, and it's not a bad idea to look for a cheap source of energy.

On our first trip we took the drilling pipe (over a mile of it), the small portable office building, mud pumps, generators and other miscellaneous equipment. I felt comfortable about the cargo. Robbie seemed to do a good job of tying it all down safely. But in a couple of hours we would know for sure if it was indeed safe.

The wind was fresh in the channel, and as the ship passed through the most dangerous fifty miles or so, the tide was flooding, going with the wind into the Caribbean, which made our passage relatively smooth.

"Jolly good for us!" I muttered to myself.

Arriving off Cabo Rojo, I was able to get a fix on the lighthouse. Our speed was 5.8 knots. I called the crew together.

"Men, in a couple of days it's Christmas. We won't be home but we will be stuck on this boat. I know it's a bummer, but try not to let it get you down." Jesus, why did I say that? Hell, they already knew. You dumb asshole!

We'd been out three days from Azua and everything was going well, the engines running good and the weather holding. Michael was on the wheel, and I was there with him as usual. Pimp came on watch, and Michael asked me if I'd mind him staying with Pimp awhile.

"It's okay by me," I said. It was about two in the morning and very quiet, the sea fairly calm.

"I'm going to take a nap for a few minutes," I said. "Call me if you see anything. Anything, you understand? Regardless, wake me in 30 minutes."

I had not slept in eighteen hours; I could barely keep my eyes open. I was tired and really needed some rest. Leaving those two at the wheel alone was dumb, I admit. But I thought, what could happen, give them a chance, maybe a little responsibility is exactly what they need.

We were crossing the dangerous Anegada passage, which some say is more perilous than the Mona. It is the main shipping channel between the Caribbean and Atlantic for vessels going to and from Panama.

I awoke thinking that I was in a hotel fire; sirens screaming, air horns blasting, bells ringing. What a racket! I made it to the bridge in two giant leaps to find Michael and Pimp laughing their heads off. I looked aft. About a quarter mile back was a large freighter dead in the water. It had its spotlights on us, and I knew that if the crew had any guns, they too would be aimed at us.

Pimp and Michael had crossed ahead of the freighter.

I stomped back into the wheelhouse and screamed, "Do you know how close you came to killing us all? Get off the bridge, now! Go below and stay there, damn your good-for-nothing hides. You two are the biggest screw ups I've ever known."

When two vessels meet at right angles or thereabout, the one who has the other on his starboard side must give way and let the other pass ahead. Your starboard running light is green, therefore, you must give the other ship the right-of-way.

The freighter, which I believe was German, knew we were on a collision course, but they also knew they had the right-of-way. When it became apparent our boat was not going to give way, the officer on the bridge had to wake the chief engineer, the only person with the authority to stop the engines. I could imagine the chief hustling down to the engine room and doing all those things that it takes to stop big diesels. He would still be in his drawers, probably, no time to put on pants. How close had we come to death, a matter of seconds. I could see those guys coming back on deck, exhausted and furious. Can you imagine what they must have called us?

I thought, why not turn the ship around, go back, hand over those two and say, "Do whatever you want with them, I don't care." Out here at sea, I'm the law. I could have done just that. Oh well, it was a pleasant thought.

The crew, all shook up by the noise and lights came on deck and, after realizing what had taken place, they too became enraged. Michael and Pimp made the mistake of laughing. They said it was a joke. I was above, watching from the wing of the bridge. I saw Baldhead go back inside the cabin and come out with a cutlass.

"Baldhead, don't do anything stupid," I shouted.

The two were cornered between the metal building and some big boxes, and it looked for a minute as though the crew were going to cut them up. Just at the last second, Michael opened the door to the building and they escaped. They were out the back door and hiding before the others could find them.

I went down to the deck and began to persuade the crew to cool down. Baldhead was so mad, I thought he might take a swipe with that blade at anything that moved. This kind of stuff was not for the faint of heart. My adrenaline was doing overtime.

After that episode, I never trusted Michael and Pimp to do any task without supervision again.

We sighted Guadeloupe on December 24. By the time we got to Basse-Terre, it was after dark. It took forever for Customs and Immigration to come on board. Thank goodness the agents for the French speculators, who were the new owners of the oil rig equipment, were there to help us with the necessary paperwork.

It was unfortunate that we arrived on Christmas Eve, because no one would be working, so we would have to wait an extra day to be unloaded. I guess I'd made a mistake by not staying in Azua for Christmas. At least there the boys would have had a much happier time with their newly found Spanish friends.

No one wanted to go ashore; this was a very strange place to them. Back in the Dominican Republic, the guards, the children and the ladies who sold vegetables all tried to speak English, and we tried to speak Spanish. It was a lot of fun, but not with these Frenchmen, who obviously thought quite highly of themselves, and did not speak English. Neither did we know any French.

I went out to a bar and bought the crew some beer. On the way back, I was lucky enough to also buy two five-pound skipjacks, a very tasty relative of the tuna family, at the fish market. It wasn't much, but it was better than bologna. The next day, Christmas, we lay around and slept most of the day. It was a sad and depressing time. A man named Alfred from Antigua came on board to visit with the guys. He was tall, about six-foot-two and very black. He looked hungry, eyeing some stuff left on the cabin table, so Baldhead fed him. Later, I was taking a walk when Sidney came up to me.

"Skipper, Alfred needs a job, and me and the others believe he's okay. Would you think about takin' him on? We do need help," he said.

"Sure, I'll give it some thought."

When I came back to the ship, Alfred was there and for the first time I noticed he had no shoes on and his clothes were tattered and patched. I asked him to step over so we could talk.

"I understand you'd like to work with us on this trip, am I correct?"

"Yes, sir," was his quick reply.

"Tell me about your experience on ships or schooners," I said.

"I ain't never worked on ships before, but I've done a lot on schooners," he replied. "I've been to Trinidad, Barbados, Anguilla, and all them other little islands. I can set sail, handle cargo, and steer as good as anybody," he said.

"How come you're in Guadeloupe if you're from Antigua?" I asked.

"I was crew on a schooner and me and the skipper got into it," he said. "He wouldn't give me my money. The bastard had spent it on a French whore. I was left here to starve, Cap."

"How long have you been here in Guadeloupe?" I asked.

"A week. I sure was glad to see you men! I been

eatin' coconuts and scraps from the market all week. I sure do appreciate you all giving me somethin' to eat."

"I'm going to hire you for the trip to the Dominican Republic and back, that's all. It'll be up to you to get home, you understand?" I said.

"Yes, Cap, I'm gonna do good, Cap," he promised.

CHAPTER 9

"This Old Boat Is Sinking"

The next day, the crane was there early to start offloading the ship and we were finished by six that afternoon. Just as soon as the crew would tie up a bunch of stuff, the crane would hoist it onto the waiting trucks and away they would go. Besides being efficient, these French West Indians had a very high regard for themselves. Some of the mulatto women were quite beautiful; mixing French and Negro blood produces a narrow-nosed, thin-lipped, dark skinned person with striking features.

I said, "Let's eat something and get the hell out of here." We backed away from the dock, and I set a course for the Dominican Republic. In those days, clearing to leave the French islands was not a formality, just a statement. "We're leaving."

Well, wouldn't you just know it, Michael found another convert in Alfred. It wasn't long till trouble started again; Michael, Pimp and Alfred were like three 12-year olds, playing around on deck, throwing a ball one of them found. This ball would occasionally be thrown into the crew's cabin, either by mistake or on purpose, disrupting what little peace and quiet there was for the sleeping men. On more than one occasion, fights started. Nothing too serious, just a lot of cussing and threats.

Michael continued his brainwashing campaign on the rest of crew, trying to get them to join the Black Power movement, and concentrating on George and Baldhead.

George, however, being older and more levelheaded, wasn't a good target. So 32-year-old Baldhead was it. Michael would start arguments with him day and night. Baldhead did resist. He would argue as long and as loud as Michael. Obviously he liked doing it. As each one of the crew came up to the bridge to stand their watch, they would give me a blow by blow of the political debates. Needless to say, by keeping to the bridge, I stayed away from it all.

The weather was good and the crew were looking forward to seeing their Spanish friends again back at Azua.

West Indian people love their once-a-year carnival. Some literally live from carnival to carnival, working on their costumes and preparing for the competitions (steel band music and best costumes), so much that it's almost like a full-time job. Just about everyone dresses up in some sort of costume, some absolutely beautiful, and party for two or three days and nights. All the islands have their own Calypsonians, songwriters and singers, who can compose a song about any subject. In the old days they were the village wags, spreading the current gossip—political, private, love affairs—or anything to get the attention and approval of their audience.

Pimp was an aspiring Calypsonian. Calypsos are full of curse words, and many of the songs are edited for radio and T.V. . . . well, just a little. One year the mighty *Sparrow* won the street competition with his song *Archie*. Archie was a young rebel who kept getting into trouble and being arrested, but each time this happened, Archie would get away to do some more mischief. The melody went "Archie f . . .'em up, Archie f . . .'em up." Well, this was not good for the radio or television so they made Sparrow change the "f" word to "buck 'em up." Made sense to me.

Pimp came up with a dose of a song, that went something like this: "Flash, he gonna kiss my ass, mon. I'm-a gonna take da Captain's job alas." Well, guess who Flash was. You're right, it was Baldhead. Michael named him back in St. Vincent because of his shiny head, and it stuck with the crew. This just about drove Baldhead nuts, but since there were three of them, he wasn't going to fight them all. I knew something would eventually happen.

Baldhead told me about carnival on his island when he was very young. He said everybody got drunk, and if you looked like you were carrying something to drink, you could get right in the middle of the party and have a ball. Well, he was dirt poor and couldn't even afford a small bottle of cheap rum.

"What'd you do?" I asked him.

"Cap, I carried a half bottle of turpentine, and it worked fine. I'd flash it around and make like I was drinkin' the stuff, but I was really gettin' drunk on other people's rum," he answered.

On the second day out of Guadeloupe, Michael was standing his watch, barefooted as usual, and talking my head off about how badly the FBI was treating Malcolm X and the other Black Panthers back in the States.

"Mr. J. Edgar Hoover, that great Afro-Americans' hater, head of the FBI, how'd he get that job? Mr. King and Malcolm could run that country in high style, just giv'em a chance."

From his reasoning, I got the idea the FBI was a branch of the Russian KGB. All this was going in one ear and out the other, and finally his watch was over and Pimp came on duty.

Baldhead was below, and knew the trio would be split up at this time, so he was waiting for Michael just inside the cabin. Being on the bridge and keeping track of our compass course was occupation enough for me, so I missed the fight down below. Sidney told me later that Baldhead was waiting for Michael and challenged him, and they were off. Both men were about the same height and build, over six foot and 190 pounds, but I would have given Baldhead the edge. I was right, Michael took a beating. Sidney was watching and said he suddenly heard a distinct click. Michael had pulled a switch blade knife.

Baldhead had been in several fights before; he ran to his bunk and came back with his cutlass. The advantage went to Baldhead, but Michael lunged at him anyway. Baldhead parried the swipe and could have dealt a death blow but instead, like a matador, he came over the top of Michael's head and gave him a whack on the back. Lordy, I wish I could have seen that blow; I heard it was magnificent! He had hit Michael with the flat of the blade and knocked the wind out of him. The fight was over.

I heard about it a few minutes later when Robbie came on watch and told me.

"How'd Michael take it?" I asked.

"I don't know," Robbie said.

"That's strange," I said. "Why not?"

"Before he could speak," Robbie said, "we locked him in the paint locker."

The paint locker door was water tight and had no ventilation! He would suffocate! I jumped down the ladder and opened the locker door. Michael was slumped over on the deck, his head resting on a paint can and his tongue hanging out. I pulled him upright and checked his breathing. Damn, he was dead!

"Give me a hand!" I shouted.

Sidney and I pulled him out onto the main deck. I yelled, "Do any of you know mouth-to-mouth resuscitation?"

Nobody volunteered, so I said, "Get a mirror, quick." I started what I thought to be mouth-to-mouth, pumping his chest five times, then holding his nose while blowing air into his mouth. His lips were blue-black and cold. I did not like putting my mouth on his, but I had to do it. George was holding the mirror, and after what seemed an hour, but was actually only two or three minutes, George said, "He's breathing."

In the meantime, Baldhead was bleeding like a stuck pig. In the panic to help Michael, no one noticed Baldhead had a six-inch cut on his forearm. "Damn it, Baldhead," I said. "Stop bleeding all over the place. Sidney, get a tourniquet, put it around his arm." The knife had sliced a gash about half an inch deep, and it needed stitches. I knew we didn't have a medical kit on board, because that was one of the things I had asked for but didn't get back in Trinidad.

"Robbie, do you have any lightweight fishing line?"

"Sure," he said.

"Go get it and straighten out a small hook, with a curve in it like this." I showed him the curve I needed, just enough to enter the skin and curve back out quickly.

Five minutes later, he was back with the line and hook and I asked, "Baldhead, how bad a dude are you?"

"Boss, are you gonna do what I think you gonna do?" he asked, his eyes big and unbelieving. Baldhead started to get up; we all jumped on him and after a short struggle, he agreed to stay still.

I gave him a balpeen hammer to hold on to, and George and Sidney held him while I began to sew him up. I managed six good stitches before he threw us off, screaming and cussing.

I know this kind of medical practice seems crude, but it is not an unusual story among sailors. Several years back, a large sailboat was halfway across the Atlantic, heading for the Caribbean island of Antigua. One of the crew, from England, was accidentally standing in the wrong place when the mainsail boom came across the deck, an uncontrolled jibe, and hit him just at the top of his forehead. He was scalped, really scalped, with his hair lying on the back of his neck. It knocked him out instantly, and he was lying on the deck, blood everywhere. The captain, a very level headed man, sewed his scalp back on with fishing line and a sail sewing needle. My friend was eventually transferred to a passing freighter with a proper doctor on board, and he completely recovered.

Now you'd think I'd have made a friend for life by saving Michael's life. Not so, he became sullen, his attitude far worse than before. He was showing total animosity toward me and the rest of the crew, especially Baldhead. I knew we had a very unstable person on our hands. No amount of kindness had any effect. The others had to force him to do his watches. He did his tour at the wheel in total silence, and I finally gave up trying to communicate.

We'd been out two and a half days from Basse-Terre, and we were crossing the Mona Passage at about eleven o'clock at night. We were steering west, and the wind and seas were following us. For some unknown reason, I just happened to look astern, the following seas were breaking onto the vessel. I was astounded to see the stern of the ship under water. I yelled for Robbie, who was on watch, to go get George quickly! When George came on deck, he saw what was happening, and went straight to the engine room.

My first thought was that we were sinking, but that couldn't be, otherwise the engines would have stopped. Robbie came back on the bridge and explained. It seemed George had pumped the bilges continuously but had not pumped out the aft compartments for days. They'd filled up and damn near sank us! Finally, after a couple of hours, George came on the bridge and I got a chance to raise some hell.

George said, with an attitude, "Hey, before you start, let me tell you somethin' that happened a couple of years back. I took three days off from this old tub to bury my old mother, and when I got back to work, the vessel had sank. She was lying in eight feet of water and her decks were awash. Mr. Coma called the harbor fireboat, and they came over and pumped her out. It took me two days to get them damn engines started again."

"What's that got to do with anything?" I asked.

"I'm trying to tell you that this old boat is sinkin' every damn minute of the day and night." George was irritated.

"Why haven't you told me this before? There's a hell of a lot I don't know about this old boat, you know." I was really aggravated with myself.

Still, there was no need to beat up on old George. After all, he had taken care of the situation, pumped out the aft compartments, and no harm was done. It would be nice, however, to know what was going on. Yet in real life, a captain does not meddle in his engineer's business.

I was on a course for the lighthouse at Isla Saona on the south coast of the Dominican Republic. On a good night you could see the loom twenty miles away. It was time now that I should be picking it up, but I couldn't find it. I had sailed those waters to the Dominican Republic before, and I knew the navigation lights were not dependable. The lighthouse at Isla Saona was located on a small island or reef. It was not a manned facility and was usually poorly maintained.

Isla Saona was just one in a series of small coral outcroppings which form a reef ten or twelve miles long. A very dangerous reef and I knew it. Without a good position fix, it would be foolish to plow on into the night, on a collision course with uncertainty. I told Baldhead to take the binoculars, go forward, and look out for breakers. After twenty minutes or so, he came back and reported, "I didn't see no breakers."

"Thank God for that. Did you see anything at all?"

"Well, I did see some flashin' lights, real dim. Sometimes I'd see 'em and then not." Baldhead said, his shirt wet with spray.

"What did the lights look like?"

"It looked like they was blinkin'. Three short blinks and two long ones."

"You sure?" I asked, checking to see if he was joking.

"Cap, that's what I saw, what do you make of it?"

"Give me those binoculars," I said, with a little bit of nervousness in my voice. "Take the wheel, I'm going forward."

After a while I could see the flashes; it was true, there it was—an SOS. I thought, someone's on the rocks at Isla Saona. The worst place in the world to run aground. Their vessel was exposed to the Atlantic swells and would sink very quickly. The crew must have climbed up the rocks to safety. It was another two hours 'til daylight, and I had better take the boat around to the other side where the sea was fairly calm to try to get at them.

"Go get me that big handheld torch, there's somebody on the rocks flashing an SOS. We got to help them if we can!"

George brought the torch up and plugged it into the ship's current, and I flashed an "Okay" back to them. I kept doing that for three or four minutes, till they gave me a steady light. Now we had to go around the end of the reef and come up the other side. We could be near the survivors by daylight, I thought. One thing for sure, we didn't want to run into those damn rocks ourselves.

I stayed in the bow with the big torch and watched for breakers while Sidney steered the ship at my command. We skirted the reefs at a distance of about a quarter mile, and after an hour or so we were in fairly calm water in the lee, the reef shielding us from the Atlantic waves and wind.

The people ashore came across the rocks to the other side where we were, and I could see men and women. Some seemed half-naked, and all were barefoot. We counted ten people in all, waving their arms and jumping up and down, really glad to see us.

I already knew that the water was very deep right off the reef, but to make sure I checked the chart. As I thought, it was straight down, a hundred fathoms deep. I told Sidney to back the ship upwind, in what little wind there was, toward the low point of the reef, and then they could jump onto the deck.

"Don't worry if we touch a little, just get in close enough for them to jump," I told Sidney. This looked like it would work fine, but even after the ship came in close, the jump was a bit too much for the women to make.

Baldhead and Robbie solved the problem quickly. They laced their arms and hands together and called to the people, "Jump, we'll catch you!"

The men jumped and then the ladies. There were some bruised knees and skinned feet, but they all made it. We had very little to offer in the way of comfort, but some of the folks used our bunks and all of them drank a lot of water.

The Dutch captain, who was really broken up about the whole accident, told me the story: The 100-foot yacht was on her maiden voyage, a cruise which had started in Holland, where the ship was built. The captain had navigated her extensively around Europe before crossing the Atlantic to the West Indies. They were headed north, and at two o'clock in the morning, the captain told the man on watch to hold his course, and he would see the light at Isla Saona around three. He told the helmsman to wake him at that time; then he went to bed and to sleep.

The man at the wheel never saw the light because it was not on, and he made the mistake of not waking the skipper. At three-fifteen, the vessel crashed into the reef doing thirteen knots. If the yacht had been five hundred yards further to the south, it would have cleared the reef and been safe.

After risking his own life several times, the captain got all on board across the crushed bows of the ship, climbing up onto the coral reef. They had all suffered from exposure and severe coral cuts—they were barefoot, in their nightgowns and underwear—but the owner, who was on board, had suffered even more. The five-million-dollar yacht was not insured.

Once on board, the boys helped the people bandage their feet and Baldhead cooked some rice and beans. The crew had eyed the women in their skimpy nightdress, but had kept their thoughts to themselves. Before long the survivors were feeling much better and could joke about their horrible experience. In a couple of hours, we would land all of them on shore at the mainland village where they would receive proper medical care and some food. Everyone thanked us sincerely for helping, including the owner, who I noticed cried a lot.

Soon we were on our way again, and I really felt good for a change.

"How does it feel to be heroes, guys?" I asked.

CHAPTER 10

The Truck Breaks Free

The next day, December 30, we arrived back at the dock in Azua for our second and final load of cargo, and everyone was waiting for us. Our old friend, the *comandante*, his knee-length boots shining in the late afternoon sun, was very glad to see us, so were the vegetable ladies and the little children.

"I must confess, my dear friend," he said, "you and your men bring life to this dry and desolate place. I am sick to death of hearing Carlos' damn stories. Just yesterday, he drove me mad! To shut him up, I had to slap him upside his stupid head. Now," he asked, with a big smile, "what are we having for dinner, Señor?"

The *comandante* told me later, "In the Dominican Republic, there is little or no crime. If a man is caught committing a serious crime, the police shoot. If it is not so serious, they put you in the Army. You see, our government cannot afford too many prisons. In the Army, the pay is three or four pesetas a day, one meal and virtually no work other than taking care of your uniform, rifle and yourself. The other meals can be a problem. If you desert, where are you going to go? This is a small island, no place to hide."

The crew didn't mind feeding the guards and some of the little children, and I guess we didn't mind feeding the commandant. It was a small price to pay for his guidance and protection. We found out who Carlos was—

the commandant's first officer! First Lieutenant Carlos Mendez was tall and thin, and looked like he'd missed too many meals. His eyes were sunk way back in his head, dark and foreboding. He looked ominous, and the crew never did take to him. Every day he would appear on the dock and just sort of stare at the ship. Baldhead would bring him a cup of coffee, and he would sit down on the concrete dock and drink it. I was not surprised the commandant spent so much time with us.

The loading proceeded according to schedule. It was a beautiful, sunny day, so George, Baldhead and I decided to take a walk to the little country store about a mile away and find us a cold beer. We were walking up a dirt road, and were nearly there, when four or five little children came from the store to greet us. Some knew a bit of English.

"Hey, Joe, you want my sister? She pretty good, five dollars, Joe."

Baldhead said, "Captain, loan me five bucks."

"Hell, no," I replied.

"Captain, you know the ship owes me that much," he said.

"I'll stand good for it, Cap," George said.

We were talking about the food money, or lack of it. But, what the hell, these were my two main men.

"I'll give it to you, if you can talk them into doing you both for the five," I said.

Since the blight had ruined the banana crop, the girls around there had been on hard times, so it didn't take long to make the deal. While George and Baldhead were having their fun, I chatted with the owner of the store, who spoke poor English.

"Are those your children?" I asked.

"*Si*, I have eight. The two back there," he pointed to the back room. "And those," he pointed to the smaller ones in the front yard.

"Look over there, do you think the tall one nice?" he said, nodding toward a lovely young girl who was playing with the children. She was just starting to show the bloom of womanhood, firm, high breasts and a strong young body.

"Yes, she is very pretty," I said. "How old is she?"

"She is thirteen, soon to be fourteen," he answered. "If you like, you may take her to bed. She is virgin. Capitán, it would be a great honor for me."

I was flabbergasted; he really surprised me. It took me a while to figure out what to say. I did not want to hurt his feelings, but I certainly wasn't going to bed down a kid.

"Thank you, no. But I will buy her some candy," I replied, and gave her a dollar.

The boys were feeling good on the way back to the boat. George was smiling and Baldhead kept punching him on the arm and winking at me.

"Lord, that woman's had too many babies. It was like fallin' in a well," George said, laughing. "I had to spread out my arms and legs to maintain my position!"

I was ahead of them and when I looked around, Baldhead had fallen backwards in the dust, laughing. I got started then, and we all had us one helluva time on that old dirt road: George laying there spread eagled, humpin' up and down. I doubt I'll ever laugh that hard again.

"This ain't such a bad trip," Baldhead said, after we had gotten up and started walking again.

They joked and smiled all the way back to the boat. It takes so little to make most men happy.

The loading continued all day long. The crane would lift the equipment—pipe, generators, motors—on board and Robbie would tie it down. The big Mac truck presented the greatest problem, so finally Robbie welded steel rods to the chassis of the truck and then to the steel deck. Everything looked good, but I had George check the tie-downs one more time before we left.

Finally, we were ready to go. Everyone was on the dock to say goodbye, and I even got hugs from the *comandante*. The Spanish are a highly emotional people; I don't believe there was a dry eye anywhere. I have never seen anything like it; it was as if we were all close family. Even Lieutenant Carlos was shaking hands all around. Those people were so appreciative of the crew, but what did we mean to them? I began to realize something. Until we arrived, they'd had no contact with the outside world. We were the world to them. Come to think of it, I hadn't even seen a radio around Azua. We were leaving and taking away their only tie to the outside, the oil drilling rig. Maybe I'm over-stating the situation, for they did have the occasional newspaper. Oh well, *adios, amigos*."

For the second time in ten days, we were headed for the Mona Passage. We had been lucky with the weather so far. But all this deck cargo made me uneasy, especially that damn Mac truck. If it broke loose, I hated to think what might happen. We rounded the cape at Isla Saona and headed out into the open channel. Puerto Rico was a long way away. In the middle of the channel was an island called Isla Mona. At one time, the Spanish had built a small penal colony there, and some of the structures still stood, including a lighthouse that worked now and then. That night it was working, and I could see the long beams of light at a great distance, occasionally disappearing and reappearing. That meant one thing: there were some huge waves between the light and us.

I asked Robbie to go down and get the rest of the crew. When they came on the bridge, I said, "Up ahead is some real rough water. The moon is full and the wind is fresh. This causes a confused sea, especially when the tide is ebbing.

"George, you know your job. Keep the bilges dry, if possible, and give Robbie a hand with the cargo. You all keep your eyes open and your fingers crossed: we're going to be in the shit in an hour or so. Let's be extra careful till we can get on the other side of that mess up there. It's gonna be rough, and scary, so if you see any loose cargo, fix it fast."

The wind was coming from the northeast, hitting us on the port quarter. The sea was lumpy, waves six to ten feet and breaking in all directions. The wind was fresh, picking up spindrift, the foamy spray from the tops of the waves, and throwing it to leeward. Sidney was at the wheel and I was pacing back and forth, looking forward, then aft. We had a couple of bright spotlights aimed at the cargo, so at least we could see it well. I watched as Robbie worked his way around through the stuff, checking the tie-downs, getting soaked with spray.

The night sky was spectacular. The full moon, still low in the east, was picking up the tops of the waves, making them sparkle as if streaks of electrical current were flashing about. The troughs, dark and ominous, I feared the most. The ship plunged down into them, twisting and moaning till she reared up, shook herself and sprang out over the next wave, still alive. Each time I felt good for her and me. I'd shout, "That way, baby," "That's my girl," or "Come on, you can do it!"

I was proud of Sidney, so intent on his steering. He was working the ship through those big seas like a pro. "Hey, you're doing great! Keep them waves on the port quarter," I said, just to break the silence. His clothes were soaking wet with sweat, so I asked, "You all right?" He nodded.

The next moment Baldhead came on the bridge and

told me the bow section was breaking up. Damn, wouldn't you know it?

"Sidney, I'm going down to check on the bow. Just keep her on course the best you can."

Baldhead and I passed through the galley into the pantry to get to the deck hatch, which led to the bow section below. I opened the steel hatch but that was as far as I got. The noise was frightening, and it was jet black down there. I could hear the broken steel struts crashing about, steel against steel. The hull itself was flexing like an empty plastic soda bottle. I heard water splashing.

"What's aft of here?" I shouted in Baldhead's ear.

"Fuel tanks either side," he answered, his eyes large with fright.

"Let's get out of here. There's nothing we can do. I believe the damage is done. Hopefully she'll stand up till we get in somewhere." I motioned for us to leave.

As we came out onto the main deck, I noticed that the ship was listing to starboard about fifteen degrees, and she didn't act like she would come back up. I said, "Baldhead, go ask George why she's listing, quick."

I made my way back up the ladder to the bridge. As I climbed onto the port wing, the spray nearly blinded me; the wind was blowing hard now. And who did I see, sitting right there in the little lifeboat, looking like three wet monkeys, but Michael, Pimp, and Alfred!

I could not believe my eyes. There they were, three cowardly bastards, sitting there, afraid to move. They were disgusting, I felt like breaking their fucking necks.

"What the hell do you think you're doing?" I shouted.

"We're taking the boat," Michael shouted.

"Go ahead, you dumb bastards, throw that boat over the side! See how long you last out there! Come on, I'll help you. Stupid asses, you best help us keep this old barge afloat."

At that moment, I didn't give a damn whether they lived or died. It was one thing to be slackers and trouble-makers . . .

Robbie came on the bridge very excited and yelled, "The starboard side of the bilge pumping system is clogged up, and George can't get it free! That's why she's listin'!"

The old bitch was going to sink on us after all.

I asked Robbie, "What's in those tanks back there on the starboard side?"

"About twenty tons of fuel in one, and ten tons of water in another."

"Go tell George to pump out the water, that should right her till he can get the damn bilge pump working," I said.

A supply ship has one purpose in life, to bring supplies out to the offshore drilling platforms. Its hull is made up of various tanks that hold different products such as gasoline, diesel fuel, and water. The main deck is one hundred feet long and usually carries large equipment, such as generators, pipe, and pumps. So by emptying one tank, we reduced the weight on that side and changed the ship's attitude, making her level.

Finally, she came up right and at about the same time George was able to free up the bilge system. We were going to make it! With the help of the full moon, I could see fairly smooth water two or three miles ahead.

The waves constantly threw us around, but now at least we had hope.

Just then, Robbie tore into the wheelhouse and shouted, "The truck's broke loose!"

I pushed Sidney aside and turned the wheel hard to starboard. The vessel bucked, twisted, and moaned, and we took a wave over the port side, but I got her running down with the wind and waves. I idled back the engines and told Sidney to let her float downwind, toward Mexico. This eased her motion considerably, so we could now work on that damn truck. It had broken free and come to rest against a big crate.

George had been back there on deck, and he'd jumped onto the truck and rode it back and forth across the deck a couple of times. I thought he was nuts, but that could have been the safest place to be.

The truck, being on rubber tires and on that wet, steel deck, would continue to skate back and forth and break things loose till we fixed it; otherwise it would cause us to capsize. We had to do something fast and get back on course.

"Let the air out of the tires," George instructed.

"That'll take too long," Robbie said.

"Not with this," George said, holding up a little valve remover tool.

"Good idea, but let's get the snatch block and pull her back to the middle where she belongs," I said. "Then let the air out."

A pulley was necessary to move heavy objects around on the deck. Just back of the crew's cabin we had a big winch and a long cable. To pull in various directions, we secured the snatch block somewhere convenient, tied the cable around the object to be moved and then dragged the object toward the snatch block. We pulled the truck back into the middle of the deck that way.

As George let the air out of the tires, Robbie welded a small steel plate to the deck, and then to the tire rim. All this took about an hour. When we were finished, I said to Sidney, "Now, head her toward Puerto Rico."

In a couple of hours we were in calm waters on the back side of the island. The sun was just coming up behind the mountains. Maybe it was because we had survived the night, but that dawn made the island glow. The sun's rays were radiating skyward just like a giant fan, forming a vibrant backdrop to the whole scene. The ever-present dark clouds over the rain forest were there and, as usual, a rainbow arched itself into the mountainside. This was the stuff artists and poets become euphoric about. Me too.

Everyone was up on the bridge except the three stooges, as Michael, Pimp and Alfred were now called. But we were a pretty sorry looking bunch—wet, dirty, tired and relieved. I knew I wanted to say something, but what? For the first time, I was at a loss for words. I was so full of pride and relief that we'd made it. All I could think of saying was, "Did you see those assholes sitting in that damn lifeboat?" I laughed and they laughed . . . I glanced down onto the lower deck and there were Michael, Pimp and Alfred listening to what we had said. I realized from their expressions that trouble was on the way.

Everybody was out on the foredeck, talking and joking around, grins all over their faces, acting like they had a free pass to a whorehouse.

The crew, including myself, had come through the night with only minor cuts and bruises. George and Robbie had rust stains and mud all over them from the bilge water; Sidney was drenched with sweat and Baldhead was nursing a bump on the head.

George was suddenly very talkative, describing his heroics of a few hours earlier. "I was standin' up to my knees in water takin' that damn pipe flange apart," he said. "I thought I'd drown before it let go. When it finally came open, it was like I gave it an enema! You should've seen the shit that came out of that pipe. Hell, that's what's been her problem for years. She was blocked up with rust and stuff. It took Robbie and me ten minutes just to bolt it back together. After that, I pumped them bilges down dry in no time at all. Cap, you reckon the ship would've gone on over?"

"George, I'm going to say this just once. If it hadn't been for you and Robbie freeing up that pump, all of us would be playing the harp by now."

"Except Baldhead, he'd be roasting his ass," George said, sarcastically.

Baldhead, who was being very quiet for a change, declared, "If this is seaman's work, I quit."

Robbie, whom we never heard much from, got his two cents in, too. "Did you see old George ride that truck? I didn't think the old fart could've done it. That was some ride you had, cowboy George. Did you see that old truck dancin' around?"

"I fixed her good," he continued, "She didn't move after I got through with her."

"Why didn't you fix it good the first time, asshole?" Baldhead said.

"All of you go below and get something to eat and rest," I said. "I'll steer for awhile. I can handle it in this calm water."

"You sure?" Sidney asked with a smile, his round face beaming.

I needed to sort things out. The situation was critical. The bow had to be repaired as soon as possible. It was flexing every time we went through a wave. There was no drinking water, because we'd pumped it all over-board. The engines were coughing up bellows of black smoke since Malcolm hadn't replaced the injector tips like I'd asked him to. On diesel engines, the injectors act something like a spark plug on a gas engine. There was rice and beans, and little else to eat. And I was down to my last seven dollars. What a mess!

I thought about going into Puerto Rico and calling Malcolm. Then I remembered that U.S. regulations pro-hibit any ship from coming into their ports without all the necessary papers. We had no papers, so we'd have to carry on another couple of days to Basse-Terre.

Suddenly, Robbie came flying into the wheelhouse, very excited, and white as a sheet. He shouted, "Captain, they got the others! They got knives!"

"What do you mean? Slow down, tell me," I said.

"Michael and them slipped up behind the others at the table and put knives to their throats! They said if you don't take them to Puerto Rico, they'd cut Baldhead and the rest of them."

"Calm down, take the wheel, just head toward Puerto Rico. I'll be back in a minute. Don't worry, it'll be okay," I said. I'd no idea what I was going to do, but I had to reason with those nuts. I was caught off guard. I'd never dreamed something like this would happen. If anybody got hurt, it would be my fault.

I walked into the cabin and it was exactly like Robbie had said. Sidney, George, and Baldhead sitting there, all with a knife held by one of the stooges at their throats.

"What the hell do you think you are doing? This had better be a joke, because you all will go to jail if it isn't!" I said nervously.

Michael had Baldhead by the ear. The big fucker looked mean, his lips drawn back, and his bloodshot eyes made me think he was high on dope. Talking to me through clenched teeth, he said, "You've made fun of us for the last time, cocksucker. Take us to America, and don't try any hero shit 'cause we can kill you out here, and nobody will ever know."

I was scared. The cabin was hot, and I could feel the sweat pop out on my forehead, but I didn't want them to see me shaking. I cleared my throat, wet my lips, took a deep breath and said, "All right, you win. Now put down the knives, and let's talk about this thing."

"We can talk," Michael said, "but we ain't puttin' down the knives."

I thought, I'd better give in. "Okay, here's what we'll do. I want you to think about it carefully. We'll go into Puerto Rico for emergency repairs, and after we've cleared the vessel and started to work, you all can quietly slip ashore. Once you're ashore, I'll give you twenty-four hours before I call the police, okay?"

Pimp and Alfred nodded yes. I looked at Michael and he said, "Okay, but all of you have got to swear on your mother's name!"

I couldn't believe he was that stupid.

"Look, all of you, if we don't go along with this, somebody's gonna get hurt. So I say we swear."

I looked at each man. "George, Baldhead, Sidney, and now you, Robbie?" They all nodded their heads, yes.

For once, Baldhead kept his mouth shut, but suddenly Michael snatched his head back and said, "When I'm in Puerto Rico, I hope you come after me, Flash."

I figured they had taken Baldhead's cutlass and any other knives they could find. They had the upper hand so far.

I held up my hands and said, "Let's cool it. The last thing anybody wants is to get hurt."

I took a look at the chart, and the nearest harbor on the south coast was Ponce. It looked like a fine place to repair the boat, so we set a course.

CHAPTER 11

Ashore in Puerto Rico

I knew from experience how tough the U.S. authorities were. You couldn't bend the rules and get away with it. I also knew the three stooges would last about a day on shore before the police would pick them up. The Puerto Ricans spoke Spanish. Some could speak English, but not many out there in the sticks.

We drifted around the entrance to the harbor for about an hour before anyone paid us any attention. Finally an old man dressed in a tattered naval uniform, his hair white and his skin brown and weathered, came out in a dinghy and outboard motor and inquired, "What do you want?"

"We've been seriously damaged during the night, and we need repairs," I said. "Can we enter the harbor?"

The old man called up to me from the dinghy, "I'm the harbor pilot here. I've been retired for two years, ever since the fertilizer plant shut down. I guess it's all right to let you come in, if it's an emergency. I have to warn you, though, the Customs and Immigration officers won't like it at all. You can't let any of your boys ashore, do you hear?" He was about seventy, a nice old guy.

The old man tied his dinghy off the stern and came up on the bridge. "Where you from?" he asked, extending his hand. He was a mix of Negro and Spaniard which produces that wonderful light brown skin and fine facial features.

"Trinidad," I said. "Ever been there?"

"Oh Lord, yes! Before I retired to harbor piloting, I was captain on coastwise freighters and small tankers. We'd go down to Port of Spain and tank up on oil."

"Did you like them high yeller ladies down there?" Baldhead asked.

"I'll tell you about Trinidadians, them ladies came in all colors and sizes," the old man said. "I guess I had the most fun of my life down there at Smiley's bar and a few other places around the harbor front. Caught the clap just about every time I went down there. Don't tell my wife, for God's sake." We all laughed.

Baldhead, who was interested in anything sexual, asked, "How'd you keep it from your woman? Most women are after you the first day you're back."

"Oh, I faked an injury or got drunk somethin' so I wouldn't have to get it on," he said. "The company had a full-time nurse back in those days and she'd give me a shot."

The old man directed us to some pilings and said, "Tie her up there. I'll go call the officers to come down. Be 'bout an hour." He was gone, and we waited. Michael and his boys had retreated to the Mac truck and, for the moment, all was quiet. Sidney and the others were quite happy with the prospect of these troublemakers jumping ship.

The harbor was shaped like a bowl, or maybe an extinct volcano. The entrance was narrow, very tight for ocean-going freighters, which makes it safe in case of a bad storm. Ponce is the port where the American Marines came ashore in 1916 when they occupied the island.

The village was like a picture, houses grouped around the water's edge, the small fishing boats pulled up on shore, with nets stretched out on poles to dry in the sun. It was typical of thousands of fishing villages in the Caribbean.

Over on the starboard side was an old building, a factory of some sort, which was disused, and we were tied up to the remains of its dock.

About an hour later, the Customs and Immigration officer came on board and asked, "Just what happened, and what is your damage?" These men were very efficient and I knew from experience would not tolerate any nonsense.

I told him about the bow caving in, and the bilge pump, just enough to satisfy his curiosity. He looked me straight in the eyes and asked, "How the hell did you get involved with this old rust bucket?"

"It was easy. The owner saw me coming, gave me a sad story, and I fell for it . . ." I replied.

What I didn't tell him was that most of us had come on this trip to prove something to ourselves. I could have told him that I was coming out of the bottom of a rum keg and using this trip as an excuse to rebuild my self-esteem. But you just don't go around telling strangers that sort of stuff, do you?

I kept quiet about what really happened, so the three stooges wouldn't go to jail. If I blabbed, the vessel and the cargo would have been impounded. All on board would be required to stay until the trial was over, as material witnesses. On the other hand, if we started to work on the vessel and the stooges quietly slipped ashore, the problem would be solved. They would be caught and sent home, the ship would get repaired, and we'd be on our way. Finally the crew would get even for what those three had done.

We were eventually cleared and were told that no one except me, a U.S. citizen, could leave the ship. I walked about a mile before I found a pay phone, and called Malcolm collect. When I finally got him, he asked, sort of testy, "What's wrong now?"

"Your damn boat has tried to sink on us six ways to

Sunday, that's what's wrong! We're in Ponce, Puerto Rico, and we need repairs. The bow section is like jello, and the engines are on their last gasp. I'm not moving till we fix the old tub," I said.

"Is the cargo okay?" he asked, more interested in that than the crew.

"You bet your sweet ass it is. I wouldn't want to lose that, would I?" I said as sarcastically as possible.

"Hey, Bob, we're business men. You knew what you were in for when you signed on, so hang in there, man," Malcolm said.

"That's beside the point, get up here as soon as you can, and bring money. We're out of food, and I'm out of patience."

I walked up the road to a grocery store and spent my last seven dollars on some stuff to jazz up the rice and beans. I bought some coffee, sugar, and dry milk. We would eat, but it would still be boring.

Back on board, Baldhead and George had other problems. They came to me and said they thought they had the social disease. "My belly button hurts," Baldhead said, rubbing his stomach and groaning.

"I'll get permission to take you to a doctor first thing tomorrow," I said.

The next morning I went over to the old pilot's house and asked him how I could get permission to take the boys to the doctor. He said he would go along and take responsibility.

Puerto Rican men do not go to infirmaries. They consider that those are for women and babies. If the men get very sick or are involved in an accident, they go to the hospital. Otherwise, they tough it out. When we arrived at the infirmary, free to the public, there was standing room only. The waiting room was full of women, children and babies. George and Baldhead were embarrassed, hanging down their heads, and wouldn't look at anyone. The Spanish women knew what was going on, and started to snigger. Pretty soon the whole room was giggling. The women knew what the guys had and were teasing them—in Spanish, of course.

The nurse, who spoke perfect English, finally lost her patience and called them in ahead of the women. "What is your problem?" she asked.

I answered, "We think they have gonorrhea."

"Tell them I will have to have a 'short arm' inspection to see for sure," she said.

"They understand. Speak up, boys," I said.

The nurse was tall and slim, in her mid-thirties, obviously a mixture of Spanish and Negro blood. Baldhead did not miss her good looks and smooth black hair.

"Miss, what do you want us to do?" Baldhead asked, already knowing the answer.

"Pull it out and milk it down," she said, a little testy.

Each man opened his fly and pulled out his penis, and she went from one to the other, checking for the tell-tale signs of pus.

"You got it," was her remark.

They got shots of penicillin, and were told to come back in five days for another one.

The nurse looked at the cut on Baldhead's arm and said it looked like it was healing very nicely. "But tell your doctor he should practice making sutures."

"If you mean these stitches, he did it," Baldhead said, pointing at me.

The nurse had a long look at us and asked, "Where are you men from?"

"Trinidad, the land of the calypso," Baldhead said.

This brought a smile to her face and she said, "I was there five years ago, for the carnival."

George and I left Baldhead talking to her about her stay in Port of Spain.

When we arrived back at the ship, a big argument was taking place on the main deck. It seemed that Michael was leaving, but his two cohorts didn't want to go. Sidney and Robbie were shouting for them to get off, making it plain that they were no longer welcome on board. Michael was shouting and cussing at the top of his lungs, but the other two men would only shake their heads, no.

We went on board and I raised my arm, "Everybody shut up. Hey, Pimp, you and Alfred made a deal. Why are you reneging now?"

"It's a trap! Soon as we get ashore, you gonna call the police," Pimp said.

"Well, you ain't welcome here," Sidney said.

"Captain, we sorry. We won't cause no more trouble, just let us stay on board. We heard what happens to illegal folks, and we don't want to go to jail," Alfred said.

"Don't be a fool! All they'll do is send us home if we get caught," Michael said. "Come on, don't be chicken shit!"

"Look, you better not stay here! The first chance I get I'm gonna cut your ass," Sidney said.

That quieted them down a bit now. I said to Michael, "If you don't go, I'm turning you in to the police for mutiny. I'm not bluffing. You'll go back to St. Vincent in leg irons, and then to jail."

"Hey, man, I'm goin', ain't I? Check me out when I'm high-balling them ladies in the States and you are still kissin' his ass," Michael said. He turned and walked away. I thought to myself, there goes a wasted human being, uneducated, brainwashed by an ideology I doubted would ever work.

Michael didn't understand that without knowing the Spanish language, he wouldn't last long on the island. The next day the police brought him back and asked if he belonged to our ship. I said, "Yes, and would you please send him home?" They said they would, and drove away.

At this point, I believe Pimp figured out I wouldn't turn them in, so he and Alfred stayed out of the way, always standing across the deck from the rest of us. I explained to the crew, "The only way we can get rid of those two is to turn them in for mutiny. I don't know the law for sure, but I believe they'd make us stay here as witnesses. I know they'd impound the boat and cargo, and it just isn't worth the hassle. I agree, they deserve to go to jail, but I can't see us having to stay here for the trial."

"Cap, if we let them stay and they cross us again, somethin' bad gonna happen," George said.

"I know, give me a little time to figure this out," I answered.

Malcolm arrived the next day, and I showed him around the vessel. He gave me fifty dollars for food and said he would be back the next day with welders. He was driving a Ford pickup he had rented in San Juan. I didn't even bother telling him about all our troubles crossing the Mona Passage, but I did tell him one of the crew had jumped ship.

"Report him," he said.

"He was sent home this morning," I replied.

Malcolm was very lucky. The local fertilizer plant had shut down here in Ponce, and that had left a lot of men out of work. In no time at all, he was able to hire a couple of very good welders who lived just a short distance away.

I told George to remove all the injectors and box them up; I was going to give them to Malcolm to have new tips put on. I wondered what he would say, but as a matter of fact, he took them to the GM dealer in San Juan and had them reconditioned. He then had the service department come out and overhaul the injector pumps. After that, the engines ran great.

Malcolm arrived at about ten each morning with the back end of the pickup full of stuff to load on the boat, coils of nylon line, fishing tackle and life jackets for his speedboat, and he even bought a ten-foot dinghy. I asked, "How am I supposed to get all this back into Trinidad without paying duty on it?"

"When you get back, call me on the radio, and I'll come out and get it. We do it all the time," he said.

"Okay, as long as you know. I'll not go to jail for you," I said.

"Hey, nobody's going to jail," Malcolm reassured me. "Bob, you worry too much."

"There are a lot of leaks through the hull up in the bow," I said. We were standing outside the bridge on the port wing.

"We fix that all the time. Just fill the space between the ribs and the stringers with concrete. It works perfect," he said. "You won't have any trouble after you do a couple. The crew will show you."

This pissed me off. Did he think I was going into that damn bow section and do manual labor?

"Hey, I signed on here as navigator, not concrete mixer," I said.

This remark startled him, for he was accustomed to ordering blacks around and not having his orders challenged. His expression turned mean, and I could see he was about to hit me. He took two steps toward me with his fist clinched. I stepped back with my right foot and braced myself. He hesitated, and I felt like I could read his mind, "If I hit him, he'll quit. Then who'll run the boat? But then again, he might fight . . . shit, he's six foot four!" Malcolm turned away.

His indecision was an embarrassment, because at least two of the crew had picked up on what had happened. Nobody wanted a fight.

I said nothing and neither did Malcolm. In a way, this incident helped clear the air. Malcolm changed his attitude and after that, we all got along nicely. He even brought the crew some beers.

Later that day, we were sitting around and the crew just couldn't contain themselves. They told Malcolm all about our experiences, expounding on their part in saving the people on the rocks and about the night the ship was headed for certain disaster. Each telling of the stories became more and more exaggerated until finally I said, "Hey, you guys, that was just another rough night at sea. You'll get used to it." Malcolm didn't understand the joke, but the crew and I had a good laugh.

Rebuilding the bow was a mammoth task, and Malcolm realized it after the welders told him all the ribs and stringers would have to be replaced. The crew busied themselves, either on deck checking tie-downs or in the engine room helping George.

I called my wife, who told me that the situation in Grenada was not good. The opposition party, the New Jewel Movement, had called for a general strike and it had more or less shut the island down. Food was in short supply, there was no electricity, and no gasoline to speak of.

I asked, "Will you be all right?"

"So far," she answered. "Just get back as soon as you can."

I picked up nervousness in her voice that made me damn near cry; she was alone. There is nothing as devastating as waiting for something to happen, or for someone to come home. Time stands still and imagination takes wings, flies.

"I'll get back soon, hold on. If you get in trouble, call

Bob Neelson." Bob and Jean Neelson lived on another hill nearby. I knew they would take care of Kate if anything happened.

Opposite our mooring was an old abandoned fertilizer plant. The building was metal and falling in, and the roof was worse. Obviously, it was ancient.

I met an American that day who made his home in Ponce and lived nearby. He asked if I'd like to see where he had worked. He was middle-aged, white and quite well educated.

"Sure," I said.

It was the fertilizer plant opposite our moorings. I said, "This building looks thirty years old! You worked here?"

He nodded, "You see all the steel that's been eaten away? That's not from rust; it's the hydrochloric gas we used in the fertilizer process. This plant was built eight years ago."

"Did it affect you and the other workers?"

"We're being checked monthly. So far so good," he said. "But it wouldn't surprise me if it affected the older workers."

I won't mention the name of the company, but it could be in for some hefty lawsuits sometime in the future.

Malcolm had paid the crew and they were eager to see the sites on shore. So on our third day in Ponce, I was able to get permission for the crew to go ashore, that is, all the ones with passports. Alfred had lied to me and didn't have one.

"If you get in trouble and end up in jail, you'll serve your time," I told them. "I don't have any bail money and I won't be paying any fines." Tough talk from me, but I knew from experience crewmen think twice if they know the captain won't bail them out.

On the fifth day, George and Baldhead went to the infirmary and got their last shot. The nurse said they were cured.

Baldhead was smiling all over his face and singing some calypso that I couldn't understand. Obviously something good had happened to make him so cheerful.

"George, what's he so happy about?" I asked.

"Him and that nurse hit it off, and they got a date tonight," George said. "Damn his lucky ass. I thought she spent more time checkin' his cock than mine. Son of a bitch."

The nurse's name was Maria. She was a good-looking woman, a couple of years older than Baldhead. She had long, smooth, jet-black hair, which she wore in a bun, Spanish style. Her olive complexion was not yet showing signs of crow's feet or smile lines. She was slim, with small breasts, and as a package, she wasn't bad. Her husband, who was older, had died and left her with two boys, now ages seven and nine, and a fourteen-acre farm. She'd been trained in nursing at the hospital school in San Juan, and had a good paying job at the infirmary. She was a good catch. I don't blame Baldhead for going overboard.

Baldhead cleaned up real good that evening. He came out dressed in a black suit, dark blue shirt, and red tie. I was surprised he had a dress-up outfit and shiny shoes.

"They was so pointed, he could've picked a lock with them," Robbie said.

"What are you going to do, Baldhead, take her to church?"

"If that's the only place that's available, yeah. You see, she knows and I know what we both want," Baldhead bragged.

I must admit, Baldhead looked real good. I guess the ladies would say he was handsome. He came up on the bridge before he left and asked if I thought he looked okay.

"Just stay out of trouble, you cheeky bugger," I said.

Later, Baldhead told me all the details of his and Maria's first date.

He said, "I walked up to the infirmary, and arrived just at five like she told me. I found her little white Volkswagen automobile and got in and waited. I was cool, thinkin' this was gonna be easy, and didn't she just melt when I put on the charm. I still got it. Uh-oh, here she comes!"

"Hey, you been here long?" she asked.

"No, I been here three minutes. Where we goin?" Baldhead answered. "I got lots of bucks in my pockets and a beautiful woman at my side. Let's get down and jam."

"Hold on, big boy, this is Puerto Rico. You got U.S. bucks or Trinidad bucks?" she asked.

"Man, I forgot about that. Damn, what we gonna do? I want to show you off tonight."

"We're goin' to my house. I'm gonna fix all of us a nice dinner. You know I got two young ones who got to eat. After that . . . when the kids are asleep, we can jam."

"Drive on, woman, you're in charge now."

Baldhead slid over next to her in the seat and put his hand on her thigh. She looked at him.

"Cool your motor, honey, 'fore it boils over," she said, taking his hand away.

"I can see you ain't like them crazy ladies down in San Fernando."

"Is that what you want me to be, crazy? No, I don't get stupid anymore. When you got children, things change. More responsibility, you know what I mean? Before tonight is over, you will."

Baldhead was thinking, "She sounds like my mother.

Hell, I come out tonight to get down. This chick is trying to domesticate me."

When they arrived at her house, her two boys were playing in the front yard. She introduced him as Joseph, his real name, and the three of them started kicking a soccer ball around while Maria was cooking. She asked Baldhead if he wanted a beer and he said yes. After about forty-five minutes, she called them in to supper.

Baldhead had taken off his coat and tie to kick the ball, so he and the boys washed up to get ready for the supper table.

Maria was a fine cook and she had fixed the best chicken pelau Baldhead had ever tasted, with fried plantain and chopped tomatoes in an avocado pear. Stuff he had only dreamed about.

After supper, Maria gave him and the boys a bowl of mango ice cream. "What've you done to me, woman?" Baldhead groaned. "I ain't been this full in my whole life. Your food's as good as I ever had. No, I ain't never had as good." He was dozing on the couch in ten minutes.

As she washed up the dishes, Maria smiled.

About eight o'clock, she woke him up with a cold glass of tea, which he really needed. She turned on the record player to a smooth glide tune, and pulled him to his feet. "Wanna dance, sailor?"

He answered in a deep voice, "Why not?"

They came together and began moving to the music slowly. Baldhead was nervous at first, but then he realized she was pressing her whole body against him, not holding back. He could smell her hair, her powder, and cologne. He pushed her back, looking at her, and asked huskily, "What are you doing to me?"

"Step two," she smiled, gazing at him through half-closed eyes.

"Christ, what does that mean, step two?"

"Joseph, go with the flow, ain't you happy, honey?" She snuggled her head under his chin.

It seemed that Maria must have fantasized about this night for months, maybe years. Maybe she had been dreaming of it ever since Ted, her husband, had died four years ago. Tonight, she was going to have her dream come true. It had been too long, way too long. Being thirty-four and healthy, let's face it, she was horny as hell, and now she had found a man that made her crazy with desire. Baldhead!

They had been dancing and kissing for about an hour when she said, "I'll be right back, you just make yourself comfortable for a couple of minutes."

By this time, Baldhead was at the peak of nervous anticipation. He thought he knew what was happening, but it all seemed too good to be true. He kept saying to himself, it's a dream. That's it, I'm dreaming and I'll wake up soon and be back on that damned old rust bucket.

Maria walked slowly into the darkened room. She had slipped off her clothes and into a lace nightie that left just enough to the imagination . . . Baldhead was sitting on the couch, and she knelt down in front of him.

"This is step three. Think you can handle it, sailor?" she asked, looking up at him with those big, dark eyes.

He opened his mouth to answer, but she kissed him before any sound could come out. They kissed the whole time their clothes were coming off, and even as they made love.

"Go slow," she whispered dreamily. "I want to remember this for a long time."

About three in the morning, they fell asleep in each other's arms and slept till nine. It was Sunday morning and she had to get the boys and herself to church, leaving Baldhead to his own devices.

*　　*　　*

It was the next afternoon before we saw him again. When he finally came on board, he looked whacked. His suit was a mess, his shoes were dirty and his tie was missing, but there was a smile on his face.

"Did you spend the night in jail?" George asked accusingly, looking at his clothes.

"No, I didn't. She took me to her house and made me supper. This morning, she showed me her pineapples. Her kids are great! I ain't never seen anything like it. And don't ask me nothin' else, 'cause I ain't gonna tell you no more."

Several days passed, and now we were waiting for the welders. The engines had been repaired and we triple-checked the cargo. Not much else to do except sit around and tell lies.

Baldhead had left and been gone for three days. After that first date, I knew the love bug had bitten him bad.

"George, you reckon he's coming back?" I inquired.

"Your guess is as good as mine. What do you think?" he replied.

"It looks to me like I'm going to have to go get him. You see, when we leave here, the immigration will come down and check us out. If somebody's missing, they won't let us go," I said.

"The hell you say!" George was amazed.

"That's the good old U. S. of A. You play by their rules here," I said.

Generally, West Indians have been able to go from island to island and not worry too much about passports and green cards.

"If Baldhead doesn't show up tonight, I'm going up there tomorrow and talk with him. He must know they'll catch him sooner or later," I said.

The next morning I went up to the infirmary and asked Maria what was going on with Joseph.

"We're going to get married," Maria said. Her attitude was defensive, not looking at me, pulling on her white apron. I knew we had a problem.

"You know he can't stay! The police will find him and send him back to Trinidad. If he doesn't show up when we leave, they'll know. Tell me where he is and I'll go talk to him. If he wants, I can sponsor him and he can come back up here legally," I said.

"You'd do that?" She was surprised.

"Sure, just tell me how to find him," I implored.

Her whole demeanor changed now, and she became all bubbly and girlish. She gave me the keys to her Volkswagen, and from the glove compartment she brought out a map and showed me exactly how to get to her place. I drove for about twenty minutes, turned off the road at her mailbox, and entered the jungle at the base of the mountains. The single lane road was adequate, and in five minutes, I came out into a clearing. The house was a wood frame, clapboard bungalow. I blew the horn and out came my main man, Baldhead, the love-struck kid.

He was surprised to see me and not Maria. I smiled and yelled, "You got an extra cot up here? I'm moving in!"

He put up a big front, showing me the house and the pineapple field, explaining about their plans to clear off several more acres to plant more of the fruit. The place was beautiful, with flamboyant trees, bougainvillea, bananas and a mango tree that was at least a hundred feet tall right in the backyard. Maria had chickens, dogs, cats and two kids.

Damn, who wouldn't kill for this? I thought.

He got us a beer and we sat out on the porch. Finally he said, "What am I gonna do, Captain? In Trinidad I have next to nothing, and this woman wants to give me everything. In my wildest dreams, I would never have dreamed of all this. You know, she is an easy woman to

love, too. If you came up here to take me back, I'll fight
you. I ain't goin'."

"Listen to me! I'm on your side. If you could get
away with it I'd leave you in a second, do you hear me?
But you can't do it, and I'll tell you why. When we get
ready to leave, the immigration people will be there to
see to it that all the crew is present and accounted for. If
there is one man missing, we can't leave. Then they'll go
out and find you. Hell, half the women in this village
know about you and Maria. It wouldn't take them long
to be up here and have your ass under arrest."

"But Captain, I can't leave her."

"Look, I have a deal for you. It might take months
for this to work, but it's your only chance. When we get
back to Trinidad, you apply for a work permit at the
American Embassy, and I'll sponsor you. In other words,
be responsible for you. You come up here then and live
happily ever after. Simple."

"No, Cap, no way am I leavin' this place. I ain't even
walkin' down that road. I know something's gonna happen, and this will all be a dream. I'll wake up on that
damn dirty, rusty old bitchin' boat, and all this will just
be a dream," he said.

"I gave you more credit than that. You are acting like
a kid," I said.

"Cap, here's what it is. I don't expect you to understand. I'm just an uneducated, roustaboutin' roughneck.
I was born with no chance at all. And the older I gets, the
worser my chances! I can see what you're tryin' to do,
and you know I 'preciate it. But, if I leave here, I'll never
come back . . ."

He looked up then and said, "She's coming!" He
jumped off the porch and ran down the path to meet her.
He was a strong man, in his early thirties, so he had no
problem lifting her high over his head and back down
into his arms for a long kiss. When they came onto the

porch, she was flushed and smiling. She asked what we had been doing and if I liked her place.

"I'd kill for a place like this!" I replied with sincerity. "Maria, we got a problem with your boy here. He thinks this is all a dream and refuses to leave. I've told him all the things we talked about and he does not understand."

"Joseph, Bob thinks it would only be for a couple or three months with him sponsoring you. We can wait that long. I'll still be here! If I haven't taken a man by now, you think I'm in a hurry? I can wait for you." She was holding his hand, and she grabbed his arm, giving him a playful punch in the belly.

Like I said, I didn't blame him at all.

Suddenly, Baldhead jumped up and pushed her away, shouting, "You two are against me! You want me to leave for some reason!" His eyes were wide, and he had a snarl on his lips.

"That ain't true, baby," she implored. "It's you I want, nobody else."

He jumped down and ran for the jungle. I knew we were in deep shit now. He must have gone a little crazy.

"Maria, I'd better go get the boys," I said. "We've got to find him. While I'm gone see if you can get him out of there."

"I don't think it's necessary for you to do that. Let me go try before you do something which might embarrass him."

I waited and waited. An hour passed before they finally emerged from the undergrowth, hand in hand. He was apologetic and a little ashamed of his actions.

"Well, what happened?" I asked.

"I persuaded him our way was the best, plus he had his way with me," Maria smiled. "Everything is all right now."

She drove us back to the boat. Their "Bogey and

Bacall" goodbye touched everyone who watched, and no one on board dared say a word.

On January 17, after clearing with the officials, we left Ponce. We had been there two whole weeks. The bow was rebuilt and the engines were running well. MACCO 17 was like a new boat.

We had been away from our families for thirty-five days! I missed my Kate and my bed and her cooking; I missed making love to her. However, although I'd been living under extremely bad circumstances, I'd never felt better. I'd lost fifteen pounds, toned up my body, and my liver was saying, "Thank you!" All in all, I was fit as a two-peckered owl.

George and Baldhead were over their social diseases, and back to making jokes and teasing all the others, but Baldhead wasn't quite the same. He spent a lot of time alone, just staring out to sea. No one bothered him.

Even though we hadn't been home in over a month and we had two mutineers on board, morale was very high. I do believe we were feeling our oats, so to speak. I was glad, because it isn't good to come into port on an awful old vessel you are ashamed of. Now these men had something inside to make themselves feel a lot more proud. Me, too.

CHAPTER 12

A Job Well Done

We arrived in Basse-Terre two days later, and our speculator friends were there to greet us. They asked many questions about where we had been. Had we been shipwrecked? Why had we disappeared? I'd forgotten to inform them of our delay in Puerto Rico and, obviously, so had Malcolm.

In a small seaport town like Basse-Terre, the only entertainment is coming down to the harbor and watching the ships load and unload. Since we were the only ship doing so, we had quite a crowd watching.

When every piece of equipment was ashore, the only thing left was the snatch block in the middle of the deck. The Froggies began to shout for me to send it up, but I shook my head, no. This made them mad, and they began dropping bottles, food and other junk onto the deck. I picked up the block (it must have weighed twenty pounds) and threw it up the deck. This started a near riot. They were throwing stuff, and we were throwing it right back at them. All hell had broken loose.

Finally, the police arrived and told the crowd to get off the dock. We couldn't speak French, and they didn't understand us either. We shouted every conceivable profanity we knew or could dream up.

Later, when we were alone, sitting around the galley table, the fact that we had completed an almost

115

impossible task slowly began to sink in. "Well, we've done it," I said. "This calls for a celebration!"

Baldhead let out a huge yell and started shouting and pounding on the table, "We made it! We made it!"

Robbie jumped up and started going round and round singing something in Bombay Indian which made Sidney near about wet himself. I started to laugh and we all went a little crazy, slapping each other on the back and yelling to the world, "I knew we could do it!"

"I'll be back in a minute," I said.

I walked up the street to the first bar I came to and bought a bottle of rum. On the way back, I could see the wheelhouse of the ship down by the jetty. I thought, how fortunate we are, she could have killed us half a dozen times. She'd had just enough fabric to hold together this trip. I would not envy the next crew that took her on a sea trip.

Was I feeling something for that old rust bucket? Yes, she'd worked her heart out, out there in the Mona, to save herself and us. Out there, she'd been like some great sea creature under attack, wounded again and again, struggling not to be overcome. We were her charge, and she had not lost, not this time.

Four West Indians and a Southern boy can go through a bottle of rum real fast, and on empty stomachs it hit us good. "When we goin' home, Cap?"

"First thing in the morning," I answered.

"Let's leave tonight," Robbie said. "We'll get home sooner."

"That suits me fine. Who else wants to go now?" I asked.

Everybody agreed. George said, "What about Pimp and Alfred? They left this morning, and I ain't seen 'em since."

"Okay, everybody go up on the street and look for

them for about ten or fifteen minutes," I said. "If we don't see them by then, we're gone."

I knew I would take a lot of heat for leaving Pimp and Alfred here in Guadeloupe, but it seemed only fair after all the misery they had caused us. The crew looked for them high and low, in every bar and cafe in town, but they had been gone all day. I don't know whether Pimp and Alfred had any intentions of coming back.

I told the crew to get underway.

"George, can you start the engines real quiet?"

"Sure, boss, nobody will hear except me and you."

"Sidney, when the lines have been cast off, ease her out of here real slow, we don't want to wake any of those French assholes," I said.

In five minutes, we were clear of the harbor and on our way south to better climes.

I was afraid that after this trip was over, I might be asked, "Didn't you feel any loyalty toward those men you left? Where was your sense of duty? As captain of a vessel, you had a duty to protect the crew who were dependent on you for their lives."

To this I would reply, "If and when you ever go to sea on a small craft and find yourself in a situation where working as a team is the essence of life, and you find part of your team lacking in courage or desire to win the battle against the sea and elements, then come talk to me of duty, loyalty, and courage."

MACCO and her crew were on the way home. The weather was splendid, and everyone was relaxed. It was a time for reflection. Just the fact that we'd taken on such a task was something to wonder about. I had the time and opportunity to ask each of the men just what had made them decide to make the trip.

"Sidney, you could have stayed home," I said. "What made you decide to come?" He was standing at the wheel, and when I spoke he automatically stood straighter, kind of swelled his chest.

"You know, Captain, I've asked myself that question a hundred times on this voyage. I knew Mr. Malcolm would fire me if I refused to go, but hell, I could always get another job with my cousin. I believed it was my chance to do somethin' different, take a chance, live a little. And you know what? I'm a new man. I'm really a man now, and those three monkey bastards didn't intimidate me, either. In San Fernando, I was always nervous around rough people, and some women scare me, too. You know the night you left me on the bridge while you and the rest fixed the truck when it was loose? I cried and prayed; you know why? I was scared, scared shitless, but let me tell you, I watched you guys work down there, and it made me feel safe. Pretty soon I was cussing and feeling good for myself and the men, and the boat."

"Sidney, you're a good man. Just steer for the end of St. Lucia," I said. "See them Pitons sticking up over there? What do they look like to you?"

"Well, Captain, it looks like a woman lying on her back, and those are her tits stickin' up."

"You got that right," I said. "St. Lucia is famous for its Grand Pitons. You can see them forty miles away. There's a story about them; they say those two small mountains are the last home of the fer-de-lance snake. And if you try to climb up to the top, you'll inevitably get snakebite. The snake is indigenous to these islands, and sometime in the past it got to be a pest. The elders in their vast wisdom brought in the mongoose from India to rid the islands of the dreaded snake. The mongoose did its job well. What they didn't realize was that the mongoose is by far the worst animal they could have gotten stuck with. It's responsible for killing most of the birds on all the small islands, and the chickens, puppy dogs, and any other creature it can get its razor sharp teeth into."

I went down to the main deck, and looked into the crew's quarters. George was lying on his bunk reading, naked except for a pair of bikini briefs. He was reading a newspaper from Port of Spain. I asked, "George, how many times have you read that old, dog-eared paper?"

"It ain't how many times you read somethin' that matters, it's what you get out of it. Every time I read this old paper, I find somethin' I missed before. Like look here, my second cousin died, and I didn't see this in the obituary till just now. Him and me grew up together, and now he's gone. He's got at least four house children, and a passel of yard young ones. Who's gonna look after them now?"

"George, when you say yard young ones, what do you mean?" I asked.

"Cap, down in Trinidad where I come from, a woman takes pride in her babies. If she ain't got two or three by the time she's eighteen or twenty, the other women get after her. They ask, 'What's your problem, you got some sickness or somethin'?' or 'Maybe you like ladies, is that true?' Most women start gettin' babies around fifteen or sixteen. So a woman can have a couple of children before she takes up with a man on a permanent basis. These are called yard young ones. If she gets married or lives with a man full-time, their children are house young ones. Now if she slips up and has one from a different man while she's livin' with somebody, that's a yard young one, too. Cap, the best time in a West Indian's life is when you're small. Everybody loves you, you can get food anywhere and do just about anything your little heart desires, and nobody gonna say nothin'."

"I got it, George. Tell me something. Remember what you told me that day back in San Fernando, about how you didn't like being away from home at night? What made you change your mind?"

"You did, Cap," George said.

"Hey, you make me feel good, but that's not the real reason, is it?" I asked.

"Well, it's part of it, but the main reason was what Mr. Malcolm said that day, about doing somethin' before it's too late. Us older men down here don't live much past our fifties. Oh, you see the odd 'old fellow' with white hair and bent over his cane, but usually the rum and the women and the clap get us before we get past sixty."

"You're telling me you came on this damned old boat because of that?" I said.

"Cap, how many places you ever been, hundreds, thousands? Before this trip, I'd been to one, Trinidad. Now I can talk about my adventures on the high seas! The time I was near 'bout shipwrecked, the time I saved the ship by fixin' the bilge pump. Cap, I'm gettin' old, and gettin' sick ain't gonna be so bad now. You and Mr. Malcolm did me a big favor and you don't even know it, and I thank you."

Robbie and Baldhead were fishing off the stern, wearing cutoff shorts and no shirts, cutting up, acting the fool.

"You guys getting a suntan?" I asked.

"Well, don't you think we need it?" Baldhead replied, flexing his chest muscles.

They were catching skipjacks and mackerel as fast as they let the bait out. Trouble was, a big old barracuda was back there taking their fish every time they caught one. The barracuda would wait till they hooked a fish, swim up alongside it, and bite off the body just back of the head, leaving the head and the hook.

Baldhead was saying, "Robbie, when you hook him, you got to get him in before the 'cuda can eat him."

"Hell, I know that! You're so damn smart, how you gonna keep the 'cudas away?" Robbie said.

"Watch this." Pretty soon Baldhead had a mackerel, and he suddenly turned with the line over his shoulder and ran up the deck as fast as he could go. He had caught the big barracuda off guard and outran him. The fish plopped onto the deck. Baldhead had caught a two-pound mackerel.

"You gonna give me a piece, aren't you?" I asked.

"Don't I always take care of you, Cap?" Baldhead, being the ship's cook, had indeed taken care of all of us.

Baldhead and I were up by the crew's cabin; he was cleaning the fish and I was watching. "Let me ask you something. You didn't have to make this trip, did you?"

"Oh, yes, I had to come! I was broke and this was the only job I could get anywhere," Baldhead said.

"You're telling me a man of your abilities can't get a job?" I said.

"Captain, I've worked all over Trinidad, and most of Tobago. People who know me say I ain't no damn good, and it's true. I've got a bad reputation for drinkin', fightin' and layin' out with women. All you ever saw of me was the good side, and I'm glad of that."

"You're talking trash! You think I wouldn't have known by now if all that was true?" I said.

"If you hang around mean people, you gonna act mean, just to protect yourself," he replied. "I'm here to tell ya, when I gets goin', I can be one bad asshole. Not up front mean, I'm sneaky mean. I don't even want to tell you some of the things I've done."

"You ever been in jail?" I asked.

"Where you think I'd been 'fore you came along?" he answered.

"Damn, you're just a dumb fucking jailbird. If I'd known that, I wouldn't have made the trip," I said.

"Mr. Bob, don't say things like that, you don't mean that, do you?" His voice was low and cracking.

"Baldhead, you're one mean son-of-a-bitch, and I know it. But I got you good that time, didn't I?" I said, laughing.

I walked back to the back end of the boat where Robbie was fishing. I watched him for a while, and he kept losing fish. That big old barracuda, or his brothers and sisters, were getting fat.

Robbie looked over at me with a bewildered expression on his face and asked, "How do they know exactly where the hook is?"

"You ready to catch that big bastard?" I asked.

I'd done quite a bit of sports fishing, and I knew one trick to play on this old barracuda. Robbie had bought some ballyhoo as bait. These little fish are about six or eight inches long with a spear for a nose; they look exactly like a very, very small marlin. They're excellent for trolling, because the spear makes them swim just like live bait. The idea was to put two hooks in the bait, one in his mouth and the other through his asshole, on the same leader of course. The mackerel would swallow the bait whole, and the barracuda would come along and bite off the mackerel's body, leaving the head as usual. But this time the second hook would get him!

Robbie was very excited about the prospect. He kept saying, "I'm gonna catch your ass, Mr. 'Cuda."

Robbie rigged his hooks and let the bait out. Pretty soon he had a nice mackerel, and here came the old boy. He must have been six feet long. I said, "It's a big one, Robbie. You think you can handle it?"

"I'll go in with him 'fore I let loose," he said.

The barracuda bit off the body, just like always, but must have immediately realized that something had him. He reared up and gave a jerk that near about pulled Robbie overboard. I yelled, "Take a turn on that bollard, wrap the line around it, Robbie, before he does take you in!" Robbie took a turn, then he could take in line or let it out. He played that fish as good as any man would have with a five hundred dollar rod and reel.

Baldhead came running down to help. "Let me take him, Robbie! You're too small to handle that big ol' bastard."

"Go to hell! I caught him and I'll bring him in, so piss off," Robbie yelled over his shoulder as he worked the fish in and out, back and forth. 1 was really impressed with Robbie's fishing technique.

The three-foot-high steel bulwark that surrounded the rest of the main deck did not enclose the stern of the vessel, so Robbie pulled the fish straight over the stern. "He'll weigh thirty pounds at least," I guessed.

Baldhead was elated. He shouted, "We gonna eat fish tonight! How'd you hook him? Tell me!"

Robbie just smiled and said, "Ole' son, that's the way we catch 'em where I come from."

After Baldhead had dragged the fish up the deck, I had a chance to ask Robbie, "What made you come on this trip?"

"I have to go where my job takes me." Robbie, usually quiet, was not muscular, but rather slim, you might even say delicate. Not that he was weak, he just looked that way, like he could do with some of mamma's good old home cooking.

"You know this old ship as well as anyone. Are you saying it didn't matter that she was old and unseaworthy, you would go anyway?" I asked.

"I'm East Indian, and in Trinidad the blacks keep us down. I have a good job and I don't want to lose it. Yes, I knew the ship was bad, but I figured if you were goin', I would too. Down here it's hard to get a job which has some technical side. You know what I mean?" Robbie asked.

"I know exactly what you mean. Stick by old George and learn all you can from him. He's your friend and that isn't bad. One day you'll be an engineer on a fine vessel, I know that! Tell me how the blacks keep you down, Robbie," I said.

"The country is run by blacks," he said. "The laws are enforced, and most of the bigger companies are owned by them. My father was an indentured laborer. By the time I was big enough to know him, he was old and sick, not in years, but in body. He dedicated his life to me, so I would have the chance he didn't. Captain, does that make sense to you?"

"Hang in there, Robbie, you'll make it," I said.

It had been a good day, and the evening was shaping up to be something special. As usual, the western sky had a thin band of low clouds trying to mess up the sunset. Today was no exception. The sun was behind those thin clouds, just above the horizon. All around, the sky was turning a brilliant red, reflecting off the clouds, fading to lighter reds, oranges and yellow streaks. High above the sunset was a light mauve then deep purple. As the sun sank lower, showing below the low clouds, it looked like a ball of fire, and just as the last possible glimpse of the red ball descended from view, there was a green flash of light. I'd seen it many times. The ultraviolet light crosses the atmosphere at a certain angle at this moment and breaks up the spectrum that causes a momentary flash of green.

We sure had a feast that night, fried fish and boiled potatoes with onions fried in with the fish. Sounds greasy, but good. I liked the barracuda myself; when they're big you don't have to bother with bones. Some people are afraid to eat barracuda, but this far south we didn't have to worry about poison in the fish.

We were a family now, everyone knowing he could do his job and proud of it. I even got out a chart and showed Sidney how to plot compass courses. I think he could have learned too, if I'd had more time to help him. I wondered what would happen to them once this was all over.

I decided to stop in Grenada to see Kate. She would be desperate by now. I felt bad about leaving her there by herself during those last days. Under any other circumstances, I would have returned home, but she did tell me she was all right, and not to worry. Besides, I had an obligation to the boat and the men. Anyway, I'd be glad to see her.

Sidney spotted an open boat to the west of us that looked as if there were men in it. I thought it looked like a whaling boat from Bequia.

"Look, Cap, they're waving a shirt or something," Sidney said. "Do you think they lost their ship?"

"Let me have a look with the binoculars."

I got out the binoculars and saw that they were waving at us, six white men at the oars and a seventh back by the outboard motor. Four were slumped over their oars sleeping and two were rowing. The wind and the sea were up and the boat wasn't going anywhere. "Whalers," I said out loud. They were headed toward Bequia, but the wind and sea would not let them make headway. They would normally chase whales to windward; that way, if they caught one, they could sail home downwind. I thought that probably something was wrong with the outboard motor.

"Head over there and we'll find out what the problem is. My guess is the motor isn't working."

When we finally arrived, the other men had roused themselves and were very glad to see us. A young guy jumped on board and we tied them off the stern and headed for Bequia, about ten miles away. The man's name was Ortin King, and, lo and behold, he'd been my first mate on the schooner for three years. Everyone called him Brother.

"Brother, how've you been? I thought you were in the States working with Dudley," I said.

"I came down here on vacation and decided to go out with these men to have some fun, and now this happens," he said.

Back in '62 or '63, Brother was crewing for his uncle on one of the family trading schooners. They had just offloaded some fruit—bananas, mangoes, oranges—in Martinique and were taking on ballast, which consisted of four truckloads of gravel and forty barrels of sea water. This extra weight down in the bilge would prevent the ship from rolling over. When they finally finished and got the ship underway, everything went well till they were out into the open channel and began experiencing heavy seas.

They found that the vessel obviously didn't have enough ballast to hold her steady. She began to roll back and forth, back and forth, finally turning upside down! The crew clung to the up-turned hull until the trapped air was gone, then they swam away using pieces of wood for flotation. Brother and his uncle were together for about an hour when his uncle began to cramp up, and he became sick from all the saltwater in his stomach. He begged Brother to help him, but Brother knew if he got too close, his uncle would drag him down also. He swam away, leaving his uncle to die!

He was in the water thirty-six hours. That much soaking in saltwater does strange things to your skin. Dozens of little fish began to nibble on his body with sharp teeth. Birds found his head a very nice resting-place. They began to fight over who would rest there next. Soon the birds were pecking his scalp and face. The sun roasted him, and he'd already found trying to swim useless.

An old Frenchman sitting up on the side of a hill

looking for sea turtles spotted him and mistook him for a turtle. He rowed out nearly a mile to investigate. He found Brother balled up, sinking and rising, in the last stages of drowning. The old man pulled him into the boat. He'd drifted over twenty miles.

When it was over, he remembered very little of his experience. Brother was in a French hospital for thirty days recovering from exposure. During that time, he got religion, believing the Lord had saved him and him alone, from the ship. He refused to go back on the sea again for eighteen months.

These men in the open boat had been out for three days fighting a whale. The whale had towed them all over the sea and then broken away, leaving them many miles leeward of their home, Bequia. Brother told us they'd been rowing for two days and were worn out. I was right about the outboard motor; the carburetor had leaked out all of their gasoline before they noticed. These men were descendants of a group of white settlers who had fled England during the early 1800s and came to Bequia to practice their own brand of religion. The group settled on the hills overlooking the harbor at Admiralty Bay and also the ocean to the east. They named their settlement Mount Pleasant. These people did not advocate slavery but, even so, there was always friction between the whites living on Mount Pleasant and the freed slaves living around the harbor. They would not integrate with the blacks until as recently as World War II. Now there were many blond-haired Negroes on the island.

We dropped the Bequians off in Admiralty Bay and headed down south. Before we left, they gave us some goat meat and fruit for helping them out. The men were not accustomed to rowing the heavy boat. Since the advent of the outboard, many men have forgotten what hard work it can be. Those were the last native whalers left in the West Indies and they were slowly disappearing.

In the past, lookouts would be stationed atop Mount Pleasant with spy glasses, to search the ocean out to the east of the island. They would only go after a whale that was to the east or windward of them. After the capture, the whale would be lashed to the long boat and the sail set. Whale and boat would sail home to Admiralty Bay. These men had made the mistake of letting the whale drag them to leeward of the island, knowing that it would be very difficult to get back home, even with the outboard motor.

Bequia had once been a favorite stopping place for Nova Scotia schooners. These big sailing vessels would make an annual voyage to the Caribbean, usually during the bad winter months, to get away from the deep freeze up north. Their cargo was fish and ice. Bequian were famous in those days for their boatbuilding skills. When the big Nova Scotia schooners needed repairs, they got them in Bequia. The Nova Scotia schooners took rum and sugar back north, and sometimes they would take fruit, like bananas and mangoes. For years, this was a thriving trade, but with the decline of the big sailing ships, the trading disappeared.

We were opposite the Grenadines now and the day was sunny and bright, with just a few puffy clouds in the sky. Baldhead and Robbie were up on the bridge pestering me to let them go ashore on one of these little islands and mess around for an hour or so. I wasn't too thrilled with the idea.

George came on the bridge about that time and said he had a cousin living on Carriacou. He hadn't seen him or his family in eight years. Well, Robbie and Baldhead jumped on me and wouldn't let up till I said we would visit for a few hours. Chatham Bay was located on the south end of the island. I said we would pull in there and if any of the Customs and Immigration officials asked, we would tell them we had cleared in Kingstown.

As we entered the bay, I had to remember the reef right in the middle. I said to myself, stay to port. Too many yachts hit that damn reef, although it had never caused a sinking or any severe damage, simply because the vessels were going very slowly into the anchorage or just getting underway to leave. Still, it was embarrassing to get stuck.

On the Thames, back in merry old England, where I first learned my basic piloting, I was always running aground in the mud. I had begun to think I was stupid when an old veteran gave me a simple little piece of philosophy. He said, "Sonny, till you run aground in the mud a few times, you ain't been anywhere. You can't be shy, but don't be too bold, either."

We anchored off the beach in Chatham Bay and, as usual, we immediately became the center of attention. Bumboats were selling fish, bananas, green coconuts and the best little delicacy in the Caribbean—horse oysters.

Ten years ago, I had sailed into this bay with my schooner and was approached with, "Hey, Cap, you want some 'icturds'?

"I asked one of the crew, "What's he saying?"

Brother King replied, "Oysters. He wants you to buy some *horse oysters*, which grow on trees."

That was a new one on me. I said, "This I've got to see, son. Go get me some and bring back the tree so we can all see it."

The crew had a good laugh over this and I, being new to the Caribbean, didn't want to show my ignorance, so I kept quiet. The young boys paddled off on their homemade raft toward a mangrove swamp and disappeared. In ten minutes they were back with a mangrove bush. I said, "Where are the oysters?"

The youngster held up the bush, and on the trunk were dozens of oysters clinging to the trunk all around. Brother King said, "Son, clean about twelve and put 'em on a half shell for the captain."

With both of the boys working, this took about five minutes and they handed the oysters up to us on board. The mother-of-pearl on the inside of the shells was exquisite. The little boys placed the small oysters on the mother-of-pearl, and everything was nice and clean. It looked good enough to eat.

Brother said, "Squeeze some lime juice on them before you try it."

If those little boys could have set up shop in the best restaurants in New York City, they could have charged ten dollars a whack for those gastronomic delights. Every time I came into Chatham Bay after that, I always had some *icturds*, which grow on trees. I played the same old trick on scores of charters, but after they tasted the little morsels, my joke was always forgiven. Chatham Bay was a marvelous place with a nice beach, a quite safe anchorage and a fine village where our charterers could walk about in a natural setting without being part of the tourist scene.

The bay also had a careenage where boats were pulled over for repairs and painting. To careen a sailing vessel, the first thing is to remove the large stones, which are used as ballast, from its bilge so that the ship is sitting very high in the water and is very unstable. Block and tackle are fixed to the top of the main mast and then to a very heavy anchor, which is attached to the bottom of the mangrove roots. Using the tackle, the vessel is careened over on its side. Naturally, they stop pulling before she goes all the way over.

Another interesting thing the locals did with their sailing schooners was, just prior to a hurricane hitting an island, to take all the schooners into the mangrove swamps and tie them to the bushes. When the storm hit, the bushes and trees would protect the vessels and not allow them to be blown up on the shore.

CHAPTER 13

Jackiron

Everyone went ashore at Chatham Bay except me. I was told to watch the boat. See what familiarity will do! But it did give me a chance to think about my wife and what our future on Grenada would be.

One thing was for sure. The Communist party on Grenada was definitely growing in strength, and everyday they were doing something to irritate Premier Gairy's house of cards. The British government had promised complete independence in the spring. Well, spring was near enough now. The New Jewel Movement (the Communists) was going to make its presence known before independence was declared. Kate and I would probably have to move to another island.

Suddenly, Baldhead came rowing out to the boat, all excited, and said, "Captain, you won't believe this! The whole damn island is stoned! Men, women and children, even the animals. That's right, everything that breathes is stoned!"

Turns out the police constable (they have only one) found eight or ten bales of illegal marijuana and, like a fool, set fire to them. The smoke drifted over the village and caused, as Baldhead put it, a "knock-out party!" Even people living to windward of the smoke came to town to see what was going on, and became high.

"Come on, let's go!" Baldhead said.

I got into the dinghy with Baldhead, and we rowed

back to shore. Little kids were coming up to me asking, "You wanna buy some 'hemp'? Good stuff, fifty cents, BeeWee (British West Indian currency)."

He was right about the condition of these islanders. They were having a party. Radios blasted out calypso music, people were dancing and singing in the road. Even the ladies in white were joining in. Hell, this was plain and simple debauchery, sacrilege. Give me some . . . no, just breathe.

I knew if we were ever to get out of there, I would have to drag those men back to the boat. I saw Sidney and Robbie cavorting with some girls and asked them where George was. Sidney had a big smile on his face and a blank look, so I said, "Robbie, you look okay. You and Sidney help me find George. We got to leave."

I was beginning to enjoy myself when someone handed me a bottle of rum and I took a swig. I should have known, it was *Jackiron*, the locally made stuff.

Most rum is distilled to about one-hundred-eighty proof. If you run it through the still a second time, you get a higher proof. The Jackiron you buy has been cut with water by one-third, leaving it in the neighborhood of one-twenty to one-thirty proof. If you swallow just one mouthful you become instantly drunk, unless you're a local; anyone who says otherwise is lying. You feel it go down to your stomach. It burns and then a distinct glow radiates out from your belly, and you're inebriated. I don't mean falling down drunk!

Robbie came over to me and said "Cap, I've found him. He's over in that house on the side of the hill." We walked over and there he was, obviously dead drunk; he had passed out. He was laying half on and half off the bed. Another man was in a similar position on the other side. There was a empty bottle of Jackiron lying on the dresser. The house was a mess. In the tropics, a house is used mostly for sleep and shelter from the rain since it never gets cold. I could see through the walls and there were no windows, just window openings. The cooking is done outside; bathing is down by the sea.

"Come on, George, we got to go home." I pulled on his arm to get him up on his feet. He objected to this treatment and muttered something I couldn't understand. His legs were like rubber, and it was obvious he couldn't walk. I let him back down into the chair. I was beginning to get high myself, so I knew we must hurry.

"Robbie, what the hell are we going to do? We have to get going," I said. We were a half a mile from the beach and over rough ground to boot. We couldn't carry him.

"I've got it," Robbie said. "Look over there, there's a barrow. We can wheel him down to the beach."

George was totally out of it. We sort of draped him in the wheelbarrow and off we went. It's a good thing he was drunk, because that was one rough ride. The main thing was to get him back. We finally dragged him on board and got him into his bunk. Thank goodness he was small. Now, where the hell were Sidney and Baldhead?

"Robbie, can you start these engines?" I asked.

"Sure, no problem," Robbie said.

"Get her ready to go, and I'll go find those other two."

I rowed back to the beach and went up the hill to see where they were. The air was heavy with the smell of pot all over the island. Even if people had wanted to get away from it, they couldn't. I kept asking until finally I found them—with a couple of girls! I should have known. They were finished with what they had been about and I asked, "You two able to walk?"

"Sure, Skip, where we goin'?" Baldhead answered with a look of disdain. "You want a little screw? They're nice," pointing toward the ladies. I'm sure Baldhead, had he been sober, would not have laid the girl.

"We got to get moving south. You know, to Trinidad? That's where you want to be, isn't it?" I asked. "Sidney, get up and help me with this asshole. Come on, up and at 'em."

Sidney was at least half-sober. Between the two of us we got Baldhead back to the boat. We hauled in the anchor and were finally underway.

We passed through Kick-em Jenny, a rough channel when the current was ebbing, but without the deck cargo, I didn't sweat it.

We passed real close to a big, tall rock, called Isle de Ronde, the nesting place for thousands of *gooney birds*. As we went by, the birds decided to take flight, and what a noise! It was like a huge brown cloud had passed over and blocked out the sun.

I could see the north end of Grenada now, the high cliffs, with breakers on the rocks below. These cliffs are called Carib Leap. It is where the last of the Carib Indians, the original Indians, had taken their lives. The French colonists, who beat out the Spanish, told the Caribs they were slaves and had to go to work. The Indians decided they would rather die than be slaves to the French, so they came out to the cliffs and jumped to their death.

As we drew even with the end of Grenada, up on the side of the mountain was a bright red patch that covered five or six acres. It took me a while, but finally I realized it was the flamboyant trees in full flower. Now that's something to see, with the trade winds blowing through, making them sway like wheat fields out west.

Grenada is the southern turn-around point for charter boats. Kate and I used to make it our home away from home, and we had lots of friends ashore. It was a paradise. There were many Americans, English, Canadians and others from all over the world living there, some full-time and some part-time. They could own a beautiful home and have servants for a lot less money than it took in the States. It wasn't exploitation. The foreigners were paying higher wages than the locals paid their own people, as well as providing jobs they normally would not have had.

CHAPTER 14

A Coup in Grenada

We arrived at St. George's, Grenada in the middle of the afternoon on January 22, 1974. St. George's' Harbour is believed to be an old volcano crater, and the town is built on the slopes of the extinct volcano. Therefore, there is very little flat land, where the majority of the stores and the market are located, before the ground starts to rise precipitously.

I could see people running about, waving their arms, obviously in panic. Those crowds were everywhere! The further into the harbor we went, the more I realized something was happening.

I told Sidney to look out, because there was trouble ahead. We slowed down and watched. Gunshots rang out, and people panicked and ran. Some were trampled, and some jumped into the water of the lagoon. I watched a man swim across the harbor and try to climb up on a raft of some sorts, when right in front of my eyes a red spot appeared on his back.

I yelled to Sidney, "Did you see that? He's been shot in the back! Turn the boat around and let's get the hell out of here, now!"

"You got it, Captain. I don't like the looks of this at all."

The crew was told later what happened. It seems Eric Gairy, who was an autocratic leader (a fancy word for dictator), had over the past few months spread fear

137

upon the local population of Grenada. His police, special forces and a band of thugs called the *Mongoose Gang* were terrorizing people, beating on innocent folks, staging midnight raids, making false arrests. The object of his actions was to cool down his critics, eliminate the left wing party (the New Jewel Movement) and make a false effort at showing the world what a benevolent kind of guy Eric was. What he was, was a greedy, egotistical little bastard who would do anything necessary to stay in power so he could continue to steal from his people.

If Michael had been there, he would have joined immediately the New Jewel Movement. The situation in Grenada was a bad one. On the one hand, you had a dictator squandering the country's money and, on the other hand, an out-and-out communist takeover attempt backed by Cuba and Russia. As in the case of Michael, communism was never mentioned at rallies, only, "Let's get rid of the authorities." A lot of innocent people bought that line.

When we arrived, we witnessed the murder of the father of the leader of the New Jewel Movement, Maurice Bishop, and the wounding of two others. I decided to go around to the south coast and anchor the boat. Then I could visit my wife Kate to see how she was doing. This was illegal, of course, as I was supposed to clear with Customs and Immigration before going ashore.

As we headed down toward Point Saline, we were running parallel to one of the best beaches in the Caribbean, Grand Anse beach, which is about three-quarters of a mile long. The sand there is snow white, lined with palm trees, and behind them are several very luxurious hotels. We could see the empty hotels along the beach. No tourists now, with the country in the middle of a general strike. We carried on around the coast till we came to Westerhall Bay, and I said, "Let's go in there and anchor." There were a few yachts on anchor, and naturally I asked them how things were. Their reply was, "We're leaving tomorrow." I was not encouraged.

"I'm going to see my wife and I'll be back as soon as possible," I told the crew. "If any trouble comes this way, get the hell out of here and head south. You'll see Trinidad in twelve or fourteen hours. Don't worry about me. I've got a lot of friends on this island."

Baldhead said, "Captain, can I come along, just in case you need me?"

"Thanks," I said, "but I can't let you do that. If you got hurt, I'd have a lot of explaining to do. It's best you all stay together and protect the vessel. I'm going to give you a time limit, say three hours. If I'm not back by then, you get going to Trinidad, you understand?"

Baldhead rowed me ashore, and I started walking. The guys on the other yachts said I'd probably have to walk because there was a real shortage of gasoline. It was about three miles to where I lived, and I finally turned off to go up to our place. We rented a very comfortable apartment, high up on the mountainside overlooking the harbor. Originally it had been a gun emplacement, one of several located around the mountainside, each with three or four long-range cannons for defending the harbor during the long French and English wars. There was also a powder magazine, which served as our master bedroom. The roof was arched in a half circle, the room was about thirty feet long and fifteen feet wide, with three-foot-thick walls, one small window and a massive wooden door. The most exotic vegetation grew all around and on top, flamboyant trees, bougainvillea, frangipani, and it was so cool that we needed blankets at night.

The kitchen, dining area and lounge were out on the battlement, which was covered with a lightweight roof but left open for the view. We were kept from falling over the parapet by a three-foot-high stone wall. The view was magnificent, and on a clear day we could see the Grenadines, forty miles away. I wished we could own it!

I searched the place over, but Kate was not home. Where could she be? I started to worry. She's all right, just relax, I told myself. After about thirty minutes, I got up to go look for her, and as I started down the driveway, I could see her walking up. Kate was an Icelander I had met and married when I worked for the U.S. Corps of Engineers, years ago. She was tall, slim, and blonde, of course, since she descended from the Vikings. She was very attractive with a friendly smile.

"Kate!" I called out to her. "I'm back!"

She looked up with surprise and relief that I had finally gotten home, and within moments, we were in each other's arms. As I thought, she had been visiting Bob and Jean Neelson, who lived over on another hill.

After Kate and I hugged and kissed, we asked each other the usual questions, "How are you? You look fine, how do I look? Lost some weight?" We were glad to see each other, and lost no time filling each other in on all that had happened while I was away.

Finally I asked, "Do you want to go with me to Trinidad?"

"I'm all right here," Kate answered. "When will you return from Trinidad?"

"With any luck, tomorrow night. It depends on whether I can get on the island hopper. Do you want me to bring anything back?" I asked.

"Yes, as much food as you can carry. I'm sick of bloggers and salt fish! How about a steak? I dream of a thick, juicy steak."

It was time for me to get back to the ship.

"I know you have to get going," Kate said, "but do you have time for a quickie? It's been a long time, matey."

"Tomorrow night, all night, and that's a promise," I

said. "Have any of the hoodlums given you any trouble? I heard they've been looting houses."

"Yes, the other day a mob was trying to get into the yard through the iron gate, but Jo MacInnis's dogs chased them away. Thank goodness for those big police dogs," Kathy said. Most all the people (rich folks naturally) who lived up there had dogs.

"I've got to get back. I'll see you tomorrow, God willing and the creeks don't rise," I said. What I really meant was, I'll be back if the airport is left open. On at least one occasion, the opposition had rolled large boulders out onto the runway, making it impossible to land.

I gave her a hug and a kiss and started walking back. Sam, a manager from one of the hotels, came by and gave me a lift. I asked, "Where'd you get the gas, black market?"

"Mind your own business and enjoy the ride, you bugger," he said.

He let me off at Westerhall and I signaled for the dinghy. When Robbie got to shore he was all excited about something, shouting and pointing.

"Calm down and tell me," I said.

"The police have commandeered the boat," Robbie said, gesturing helplessly.

"Jesus! Just slowly tell me what happened."

"About an hour after you left, a launch came out from Stetson's marina with four police officers. It happened so fast, we didn't have a chance to get the anchor up and leave like you said. They caught us off guard, Cap. I swear, we never had a chance," Robbie said.

Robbie was rowing toward the boat and I could see one guard, but no officers.

"Robbie, how many guards did they leave on board? All I can see is just that one with the rifle," I said.

"Just him. When the officers left they told him he would get help soon," he said.

"When we get on board, just play along with me, and if he falls for my trick, you take him ashore to Stetson's. As soon as he goes inside, you row back as hard as you can, okay? Can you do it? He might shoot at you."

"We been talkin' to him. He won't shoot nobody, he just wants to go home. We told him we been away from home for over a month, and we sure wish we could leave. He won't shoot," Robbie said.

When we climbed on board, I said to the guard, "Major Smith (whom I knew) is on the phone over at Stetson's. Said for you to get over there fast. Robbie'll row you over."

The boys later told me the soldier had only been in uniform a week, and the mere mention of an officer by name was like a death threat to him. He jumped into the dinghy without hesitation, and they were on their way to shore.

"George, get the engines going and start hauling in that anchor. As soon as Robbie is aboard, we're gone," I said.

The plan was so simple it worked perfectly, and before anyone could do anything, we were on our way to Trinidad.

"How'd the police catch you off guard?" I asked.

Everybody started talking at once.

"Sidney, you tell me," I said.

Sidney was like a little kid eager to tell me about his adventure. "We was on watch, and we saw the launch leave Stetson's and head out with one man at the wheel. He wasn't even coming towards us, then suddenly he turns right at us and these police officers stand up. They was hidin'! That's the God's truth, ain't it?" Sidney said, looking around at the rest.

"George said, "They tricked us, Cap, and got us flat-footed."

"Okay, that's one wicket for them, no harm done.

Hell, didn't we pull a good one on them? So don't feel bad. What'd they want with this old tub?" I asked. "Were we going to be Mr. Gairy's Navy?" That got a laugh.

"They wanted us to go to Trinidad and bring back gasoline," George said. "They've run out, and Major What's-his-name said he would keep one of us here to make sure nothin' went wrong. Cap, are they nuts? That kind of shit won't work, will it?"

"Desperate times bring desperate means. Something like that. The main thing is we got away from those assholes," I said.

I told Sidney to steer one-seventy, I was going to get some sleep, and to wake me if he saw anything. I thought, this was my last night on board this old ship. I'd lay down and try to drop off. But I kept on thinking about Grenada . . . the good times we had had, the parties, when Grenada Yacht Services was going full blast. We would come into GYS, drop off a charter and have a two- or three-day turnaround before we started another charter. Everybody did a lot of work and a lot of drinking. Those were good times. One of these days I'm going to write about the heydays of big boat chartering. We had a fine fleet of gorgeous sailing yachts spread out from Antigua in the north to Grenada in the south. When we would pass a friendly yacht going either north or south, we would take pictures and the charters would exchange photos. Sometimes we'd throw water bombs which consisted of balloons filled with water, or flour bombs, that is flour in a paper bag. Now that was messy.

Sidney was saying, "Wake up, we're here."

I looked out my porthole and damn if we weren't in the Gulf of Paria and the sun was just coming up. I had slept the night through. I said, "Sidney, damn your eyes, why didn't you wake me before now?"

"Cap, when was the last time you slept more than a couple of hours at one time? The boys and me thought you needed the rest. You were lookin' a bit white," Sidney snickered.

"You dumb asshole, I am white! Where are we? What time will we get to the dock in San Fernando? Will Customs be there this early?" I asked.

"We'll beat them there by an hour at least. Them never get to work 'fore nine. Don't worry about them, they're okay," Sidney said.

I switched on the little ship-to-shore radio but got nothing, not even static.

"Does this radio work?" I asked.

"Not since I been around here," Sidney replied.

"Do you think they'll find all that junk Malcolm brought on board?" I asked.

"Cap, them guys ain't gonna find nothin'. Hell, they hardly look anymore," Sidney said.

"Do I detect a little sarcasm?" I asked.

"Well, you probably do. I don't like that guy, John," he said.

"Why is that?"

"A couple of years ago, I applied for a job with the service, and they hired that ugly guy. Hell, I was smarter and better looking. It was just because he's black. One of these days you might meet me on the street somewhere up there in the States. I might just immigrate."

Sidney and the rest of the boys were in fine spirits, knowing they would be home in a few hours. I didn't blame them, I was looking forward to flying back to Grenada myself.

"Sidney, before you immigrate, just remember, the grass always looks greener," I said.

"Where is San Fernando?" I inquired.

"See them buildings over there? That's it," he said.

We were about two or three miles away and the Gulf water was flat calm. It was easy to see the birds swoop down and scoop up some little unsuspecting fish. The big white pelicans dove like bombers from thirty feet up, looking for their breakfast. To be on calm water was quite a treat.

"Sidney, when was the last time we were on flat water?" I asked.

"That's easy. Forty-one days ago, when we left this old Gulf," he answered.

We were just about there, and I said, "Sidney . . ."

"Take her in on the port side," Sidney said, laughing.

"You're learning," I said.

Baldhead came up to the bridge, he had changed into his shore-going clothes, ready to leave. And I asked him, "Are you going to the Embassy and get those papers?"

"Sure am, Cap. I think of that woman every night. I figure I'll go back to school when I get up there, and get my diploma. She asked me to run the farm, experiment with pineapples. I'd love to do that. What do you think, can I learn to be a farmer?"

"If that's what you want, you can. She can teach you most all you need to know," I said. "Have you called her yet?"

"She don't have a phone," he answered. "I'll send word to her as soon as I get home. Besides, I'm not good as you when it comes to them pay phones."

CHAPTER 15

Return Home

We tied up at the dock and waited for the officials to come on board. They arrived promptly at nine, cleared us, and didn't even ask where we'd been. Malcolm was there. He looked around, then left without saying a word to me. I thought, does he know everybody dislikes him? Can he tell? He probably gets the same reaction everywhere he goes.

The boys were taking off, and farewells were passed back and forth, a lot of back slapping and joking around, but when we each shook hands, it was a good, honest shake. Our eyes met and, without saying, it was understood, "You are my friend. Good luck and God bless."

I surely would miss this bunch.

I went up to Malcolm's office, and the girl out front said he would see me in a while. It was after lunch before the bastard let me in. I waited over two hours before he had time for me.

I never understood this, but when I went into his office, he let me just stand there. No greeting, no "take a seat," just "How much do I owe you?" he asked, showing complete disinterest.

I returned his attitude with a stony indifference. "Hell, I don't know." I was getting more and more irritated as I stood there. I thought, after what I've gone through for this bastard, surely he could ask me to sit down. He was treating me like one of the deck hands, like I was supposed to say, "Yes sir, no sir, three bags full, sir."

Finally I said, "It's forty-one days at seventy-five a day, that's $3075. Give me $2500 . . ."

Malcolm counted out twenty-five one hundred-dollar bills and slid them across the desk. I picked them up, turned and walked out. Neither one of us said another word.

Now, say what you like, but I still had enough kid in me to think I'd accomplished something special, and that the guys and I should have been congratulated. I took it very hard that Malcolm was so hostile. I thought that he and I could have buried our differences and shaken hands. It was the money; he was afraid I wanted more. So be it, as far as I was concerned, to hell with him.

How surprised I was when out in the main office, I met his wife and her sister, two very attractive women who were both eager to congratulate me on a job well done. You would think I had just come back from fighting in North Africa or something. Malcolm's wife volunteered to drive me to the airport, and I promptly accepted. We piled into her car. She drove, her sister sat beside her, and I sat in the back. All the way to the airport they both chatted about this and that. I asked them to stop at a supermarket so I could buy groceries to take back to Grenada. The ladies helped me, and it didn't take long before I had two large paper bags filled with goodies—beef, eggs, cheese and other things. I'd not tasted any of these delicacies in forty-one days.

At least I had two fans. Our goodbyes were warm and genuine. The ladies left me at the airport, and I set about getting a ticket. I caught the last flight out and was back in Grenada by five that afternoon. When I arrived, I grabbed a taxi driver I knew, Frank, and we set off over the mountains for St. George's.

Frank, who had been in the taxi and tourist business

for fourteen years, filled me in on what was happening. The shooting yesterday of Maurice Bishop's father was meant to put the fear of God into everyone connected with the New Jewel Movement, to stop the agitation, and to bring the people back into line. Somehow Premier Gairy had to break this strike. It was imperative for him to make this happen. Gatherings were broken up and marches were disrupted. His Mongoose gang had beaten up a lot of folks, yet still the general strike continued on day after day. Didn't they realize the tourists would not come, the hotels would be empty, and the island would be getting independence soon? Independence! That was what Eric really wanted, to get rid of those pesky British, always meddling and asking questions that were none of their business. When they were finally gone, glory hallelujah, then *Uncle G* would have his own way.

Frank, the taxi driver, was neither for nor against the New Jewel, but he was getting tired of Gairy and all his squandering—his hotels, his trips, his fancy women. The people didn't mind if he stole a little here and there, that was natural. But they were tired of the price of food going up and up, the lack of work, and of having no say in how things were being run. Also, Gairy had spies everywhere. No one could do a damn thing without him knowing. Maybe the New Jewel could change that, and we could get our island back.

I said, "Frank, how are you getting gas to run this vehicle?"

"I'll tell you, but you got to promise you'll stay quiet about it, okay?"

I said, "Yes."

"It's brought into Carriacou by schooner and smuggled down here in fishing boats," he said. "Me and Slick, my buddy, bought a forty-five gallon drum yesterday."

"Mr. Bob, look at them potholes in the road," he continued. "This is the only road to and from the airport. All the tourists have to ride over this bad road, and it makes us embarrassed to have to drive them. Gairy had the money for two years from the British government to fix this road. He spent it fixing the roads up to his fancy hotels instead."

"What's going to happen?" I asked.

"That a good question. Nobody's sure about these New Jewel blokes. They preach a lot about 'getting rid' of the establishment, but they don't say much about what's gonna replace it. We kinda wonder if it'll be any different with their establishment. What do you think, Mr. Bob? Do you think they'll be different?" he asked.

"Frank, you all are caught between a rock and a hard place. I think you need to get rid of Gairy. Are the New Jewel guys your answer? I doubt it. One thing for sure, something's got to give around here. The situation can't stay like it is without some serious trouble. The tourists aren't going to come here now or in the near future if it stays this way," I said.

We drove up to the gate at my house, and I said to Frank, "Hang in there," and gave him a twenty.

The food was good at home, and Kate and I made up for lost time in the powder magazine. I had a good night's sleep. The next morning we got down to making decisions. Were we going to stay here or get out? We decided to get out, but to where?

The problem was solved for us when the phone rang. Bill Dawes, the manager and part owner of the Grenada Yacht Services, asked if I was interested in moving a yacht out of Grenada to St. Vincent. I said, "Yessirree, I'd be more than happy to."

"Bring your stuff on down. You can start right away, can't you?" he asked.

I was so happy with the prospect of leaving that I didn't even ask what kind of yacht we were talking about. It turned out to be a 58-foot motorsailer that belonged to a Canadian who had left the boat in Bill's care for a few months.

The situation began to get complicated soon after Kate and I arrived at Grenada Yacht Services marina. Bill informed me that he and his wife and two children would be going along, then Jo and Laddie MacInnis, then some more people, until finally we had quite a boat load. I don't believe we ever counted heads. I told them to stow their bags and stuff in the cabins while I cleared the vessel with Customs and Immigration. Before we left, I got them all together and told them to take their seasick pills now, unless they were expert sailors. I knew if they didn't, they would be seasick and throw up all over the boat. Most of these people were West Indians, having to leave their homes and property simply because a tyrant like Eric Gairy could not come to terms with reality and do the right thing by his people.

We finally left the dock at Grenada Yacht Services and headed up the coast of Grenada. The day was perfect. It was hot, not a cloud in the sky. As we approached the Ile de Ronde, I could tell Kick-em Jenny was lumpy, with big breaking waves. The area, affectionately called Kick-em Jenny, was between Ile de Ronde and the south end of Carriacou, about six or seven miles wide. A lot of water was funneled through there during each tide change. I had been in the middle of it in beautifully smooth water when suddenly, without warning, the waves would be as big as houses, breaking every which way.

Today it was rough, the yacht dipped her nose into the first big wave and we had pandemonium, screams, dishes falling, sea water all over the deck. I shouted for everyone on deck to hold on. The people down below were busy holding on as well, plus they had to try to keep the inside of the boat from falling apart. An hour or so later we were through it and back into relatively smooth seas. They passed the bucket around down below a few times, and one kid got sick on deck, but otherwise they all did pretty well. Bill and I set a sail to steady the vessel and she came through nicely.

We were back of Carriacou, going north. I told Bill about our *pot* episode, which he found hilarious.

"What about his head? You know, you must have hurt his head, wheeling him down the hill."

"We borrowed a gunny sack from the same guy who lent us the wheelbarrow. As a matter of fact, George was too damn comfortable," I said.

Some of the folks had never been to the Grenadines before and asked if I could take them through. I said, "Okay, but we can't stop. You understand that we're wasting time, and we have to hurry on up the road." They agreed, so we angled over into the channel that leads to the famous Tobago Cays.

There are four small islands in the Cays with fabulous snow white beaches, and water so clear you can see if a coin is heads or tails in ten feet of water. These little island jewels are protected from the Atlantic waves by a semi-circular coral reef. Outside the reef the waves can be twenty feet high, but inside is flat calm.

I said, "Up here in the Cays is the only place in the world where there are blue seagulls." Some knew what I was talking about, but kept quiet. The rest were amazed at the sight of the birds. I pulled this trick on my charter folks for years and it always worked. It's the reflection of the sun and shallow, sandy bottom, combined with the bluest water you've ever seen. This is not something I've dreamed up. When the seagulls fly over the water, they are blue.

I slowed down. There were several yachts at anchor, and it wasn't nice to rock them going too fast. My passengers were enthralled with the fancy boats from ports all over the world, the water, and the reefs.

When I first came to the Tobago Cays ten years ago, we were the only yacht. Some fishermen came by and tried to sell us dead lobsters. I believe I was the first person to educate them. I said, "You have to bring the lobsters to the boat alive. They must crawl on the deck, do you understand?"

"Yes, Cap," they replied.

In those days, I was paying thirty or forty cents a pound for live lobsters. Back then I picked up lobsters off the bottom. Now you have to dive to a hundred feet just to find a small one.

We traveled on through the day and tied up in Kingstown, St. Vincent late in the afternoon. After we cleared, my passengers went either to friends' homes or to one of the hotels. No one knew what was in store or how long he or she would be in exile.

Kate and I turned the boat around and headed back to Grenada, arriving early the next morning for our last load of fugitives from Eric Gairy's paradise island. I did get some sleep, because the yacht had a very good autopilot. But those two trips were hard, and I certainly didn't want to make them, but I knew those people felt their situation was desperate.

Later, Kate and I rented a beach cottage out on the windward side of St. Vincent, and slowly our lives became normal again.

After about two weeks, I received a letter from Baldhead, saying he went to the American Embassy and had got all the papers to fill out. He enclosed the forms for me to complete, and asked me to please do them right away. I did. He'd heard from Maria in Puerto Rico, and she and her kids were fine.

I ran into a Canadian friend, and he wanted me to go into business with him. He had a crazy scheme to raise fresh water crayfish for the market. I would do the work, and he would furnish the money. It sounded interesting, so I decided to investigate just what was involved.

The local crayfish catcher was named Napoleon. He was a tall, black man about forty five years old, who lived alone and made his money catching crayfish up in the mountain streams. These animals are similar to our southern crayfish except they have to hatch and develop in semi-saltwater surroundings for the first month of their lives. Then they can crawl back up the stream to where they were conceived. I sent word to Napoleon that I wanted a mess of crayfish alive, and it wasn't long before he showed up with an old paint bucket half full of these creatures. I started small, with a plastic kiddie pool, five feet in diameter.

A short time later we moved to the Pink Cottage, so-called because it had always been painted pink, located on the beach by the lagoon. There was a large concrete slab with a back wall, ideal for the construction of four twenty-by-twenty-foot tanks. It wasn't long before I had a full blown crayfish breeding farm going, with big males (some weighed three pounds) and their harem of lovely females, in separate tanks of course.

We had started a new life on St. Vincent, and would not go back to Grenada for a long, long time.

CHAPTER 16

Bad News from the MACCO

I'd been home about a month when I received an express letter from Paul, the guy who had gotten me the job on board MACCO 17 to start with. The envelope contained a small newspaper article, which read:

OFFSHORE SUPPLY SHIP CAPSIZES—CREW FEARED DEAD: Thursday afternoon, the supply ship, MACCO 17, was involved in a fatal accident while loading machinery at the offshore rig Rough Neck. Witnesses reported that heavy deck cargo had shifted to one side, unbalancing the vessel and causing it to capsize. The bodies of the four crewmembers were recovered by the Coast Guard late Thursday evening. There were no survivors. The crewmembers were identified as Sidney Subhan, George Adams, Joseph Mills, and Robbie Rampa, all from San Fernando.

I was stunned. I felt numb. All I could think about was those four young men walking away from the ship, walking proud, slightly arrogant. Baldhead looking back and waving. He'd given me his best, nobody wanted his bad side. Sidney had become a man and I was proud that I had been part of his maturing. And loyal Robbie, anyone would be fortunate to have this kid around, smart and always helpful. Then, good old George, didn't say much, but when he did, you had better listen. I'll never forget his encounter with the whore in Azua.

I showed the article to Kate, she looked at me and

said, "Those men were your real friends. What are you going to do?"

"Well, I guess I'd better call Paul in Port of Spain, and find out when the funerals will be. I'd like to go."

I arrived in San Fernando just before noon the next day. I knew no one there except Malcolm, and to hell with him. I went over to the old Empire Hotel and sat at the bar drinking double rum and cokes. The funerals were all scheduled for three in the afternoon, the two Christians in one cemetery and the two East Indians in another. It was Saturday, and the market place was thick with people as usual, hawking everything from fish to coconuts. I decided to go to the Christian cemetery that was about half a mile away.

Older West Indians usually belong to burial societies. Being a member guarantees a good attendance at the funeral, and mourners are always provided. This means a lot if you are short of friends and relatives.

George and Baldhead must have had dozens of both. There were hundreds of people at the graves. I arrived at the cemetery early and walked around. It was huge, some of the headstones dating back to colonial times, and like all the graveyards I'd seen in the Caribbean, it was very well kept. I could see the funeral procession coming from a long way away, and I was able to get to the gravesite on time. The ceremony was very impressive, with preaching, singing, and a lot of hallelujahs. As soon as the two coffins were in the ground, the bands started playing and people slowly began to drink and have a good time. West Indian people believe in celebrating the dead, and the wake was going strong when I left at five to catch the last plane to St. Vincent.

I busied myself with the crayfish farm.

One day, I said to Kate, "I feel like I should go up to Puerto Rico and tell Maria. She has no way of knowing what happened to Baldhead."

"Why don't you just call her?" Kate asked.

"Well, to begin with, I don't know her last name and even if I did, she doesn't own a phone. Besides, I think she should hear it from me in person."

CHAPTER 17

Maria

"Well, that's the story, Robin. Some tale, eh?" I said. We'd been at the bar for quite a while. It was time to go back to the hotel and turn in.

On the way, Robin said, "You're right to come up here and tell Maria; she deserves to know. But I sure don't envy you your task."

The next day, I rented a car and bought a road map, then started out for Ponce, on the other side of the island.

Since the Spanish-American War, Puerto Rico has been under U.S. rule, and Puerto Ricans have been citizens since 1917 under a special constitution which was ratified in 1952. The island has changed from mainly farming to largely industrial in little more than twenty years, with help from U.S. money, of course.

On my way over to Ponce, I passed through Caguas, Cayey, and skirted the eastern end of the Cordillera Mountains. I drove up the coast and followed it right to my destination. It was an enjoyable ride, but the whole time I could only think of what I was going to say to Maria.

Ponce is highly industrial, with huge oil refineries, fertilizer plants and much more. But just a short distance away from all the modern industry, you will find sub-standard housing and public water pipes, all the things that made the poor emigrate to the States. I am told,

157

however, that emigration has slowed down as thousands have begun to return home.

I arrived at the infirmary at ten in the morning, and it was full as usual. I knew it was closed half a day on Wednesday, which was today. I thought I would be smart to wait till she was finished, so I could catch her at home.

I drove down to the harbor and looked around, then went over to the old pilot's house, but he wasn't home.

I finally found a bar, and sitting there having a rum and coke made me feel much more nostalgic. I kept going over what had happened, as if I was looking for some way out. It was after twelve. I ate a sandwich and drove slowly to give her time to get home and do her chores.

As I came up the drive, I could see young boys playing in the yard, dogs barking and chickens flying around. The house looked the same, white with yellow trim. Everything was neat and in its place.

Maria came out of the house looking attractive in her nurse's uniform, and when she recognized me, she ran to the car. We hugged, and I pushed her back to arm's length, looked at her seriously, and said, "I'm bringing you some very bad news. Let's go to the porch."

As we walked, she gripped my arm with her fingers, digging in with her nails.

"Please, tell me now." Her voice was just above a whisper, fearful.

"The ship capsized off Trinidad and all the boys were drowned," I said gently. "Joseph was one of them." I reached into my pocket and handed her the news article. She read it in silence. Her face slowly turned to a crooked mask, tears began to stream down her cheeks, and finally she sobbed aloud.

I held her for a while till the sobbing waned and then she sat down, dried her eyes and gave me a little smile. Her hands were shaking, and I took them into mine.

"Did you come all the way up here to tell me?" she asked, eyes wet from crying, unable to control her sorrow.

"I wouldn't have done it for just anybody," I said.

"You are a dear man," she said. "You will stay for supper. I insist."

"Well, if you insist," I replied. That made her smile a little.

After a quiet, simple supper, we sat around and I played with the kids. She had asked me to stay the night. At first I had objected, then I thought she might feel better if I did keep her company. Besides, I wasn't looking forward to the long drive in the dark.

We turned in around ten. I had a hard time sleeping on the couch. It was hot and I stripped down to jockey shorts.

About one o'clock, I felt her sit down by me, and I knew she was weeping. I pulled her down on my chest, smoothing her hair. Being loose, it spread out onto me. Her nightgown was thin, and she crossed her arms as we came together so her breasts would be covered. My hands were on her bare back, she was crying, her tears ran down her cheeks onto my chest and neck. I told myself, "Don't even think about it . . ."

"I have Joseph's baby inside me," she said softly. "I just got the news yesterday; now this."

Saying this seemed to destroy her last little bit of armor, and she sobbed, her body shuddering. She's losing control, I thought. Her nails dug into my chest, she slipped her arms under my shoulders and hugged me. I could feel her breasts pressing into my chest, her nipples were hard, the thin material of the nightgown not giving her any protection. She kept on sobbing.

"You must go to bed and get some rest," I said, helping her up.

"Thanks, Bob, I'll always remember what you've done for Joseph and me."

The next morning, we were having coffee and toast. I asked, "What will you name the baby?"

"Joseph, if it's a boy, and Josephine, if it's a girl. Either way it will be called Joe or Jo." That brought a smile to our faces.

Driving back to San Juan gave me a chance to think about last night. I'd read something concerning this sort of strange thing happening before, women being vulnerable during sorrow and grief. I'd also heard they were the most passionate at the height of their grieving; most would control it, but others could not.

Epilogue

Kate and I lived on the island of St. Vincent till 1977, when we moved to Georgia, and I took up my old profession. As a civil engineer, I worked for several years before retiring in 1990. We now live near Juliette, Georgia, home of the Fried Green Tomato.

Last year we were fortunate enough to be invited to the Caribbean for a 25-year reunion at a little island in the Grenadines called Petit St. Vincent. It is a fabulous resort with twenty or so luxurious cottages, all looking out onto the crystal clear waters of the barrier reef and the ocean beyond.

As we flew down, it so happened that we were delayed in Puerto Rico. We had four hours to kill before our plane arrived from Miami. I suggested we drive over to Ponce and look up Maria. We rented a car and I retraced my footsteps of years ago. Kate was enthralled with the countryside, the palm trees, bougainvillea, frangipani, stuff she hadn't seen in years. Maybe it was because she'd been away from the islands too long.

We arrived at Ponce around noon, grabbed a sandwich and a beer, and headed out to Maria's house, hoping to find her home. As I drove up the driveway, it seemed nothing had changed.

When we got to the house, it was quiet, with only a few chickens pecking around. The house had a new coat of paint, but otherwise, it looked the same. Out under the big mango tree was a weight bench that looked as if someone had been using it.

I called out, "Is anybody home?"

"Hey, I'm here! I'll be ready to go in a second," a man's voice answered. Whoever it was thought I was someone else.

I knew Maria had three children and I wondered which one it was. She might have even moved away. I would soon find out.

A big guy came out the door. He was young, slim, no more than eighteen, at least six-foot-two. His T-shirt did not conceal his muscular build.

I was nervous. I asked, "By any chance are you Joseph?"

"Yes, I am, and who are you?" he asked, smiling.

"I'm an old friend of your father and mother."

He looked incredulous. "You're Captain Bob!" he exclaimed.

I smiled and said, "You got me."

Maria drove into the yard about that time, and we all had a happy reunion. I told Joe, as he liked to be called, all I knew about his father—some of his exploits, but none of his misdeeds. Joe was so thrilled to hear me talk about his father.

Maria spent hours telling him about how she and his father had met, and what had happened afterwards. Joe knew the story by heart, but I repeated the whole thing again. Joe was going to school to learn nursing and had a job as Maria's assistant at the infirmary.

While Maria was making tea, I got a chance to talk to her alone out in the kitchen. "He's a fine young man, Maria. He looks just like Joseph."

We finally said our goodbyes and drove back to the airport. On arriving at Barbados, I called over to Petit St. Vincent. Haze Richardson, our host and the owner of the island, said to hang on, he would send a charter plane over to pick us up. We then flew to another little island called Union.

Finally, we arrived at Union Island, cleared Customs and Immigration, and boarded a 40-foot cruiser for the final leg of our journey.

In thirty minutes, we were ashore at Petit St. Vincent. Haze was there on the dock with his girlfriend Lyn, and they handed us piña coladas with hibiscus flowers floating on top. It was great to see Haze and Lyn, and all our friends from twenty odd years ago.

It is amazing how little people change over the years. There were Americans, Brits, Australians, New Zealanders, Canadians, Swedes, Icelanders, Italians, West Indians, South Africans and Germans. Almost all the men were captains or ex-captains and owners of big yachts. Most had crossed oceans and had many stories to tell.

Other books of interest from Sheridan House

ALL FOR A BOTTLE OF WHISKY
by Ralph von Arnim
A highly pressurized sales manager leaves Asia aboard a 44-foot wooden sloop with a group of friends. Their goal—dig up a bottle of whisky lying buried on the Isle of Arran in Scotland.

SHIPWRECK OR SHANGRI-LA?
by Peter Lickfold
Shipwrecked on the reef at Boddam, a remote atoll in the Indian Ocean, Peter and his wife are helped by visiting sailors and recover their yacht, VESPERA, that will take them back on a 3000-mile voyage home.

SAILING TO HEMINGWAY'S CUBA
by Dave Schaefer
"Schaefer wasn't going to Cuba just to write another story. His mission was to broaden his cruising skills and seek out the heritage of his lifelong hero, Ernest Hemingway, for whom Cuba was both home and inspiration...entertaining and informative"
Coastal Cruising

LETTERS FROM THE *LOST SOUL*
A FIVE YEAR VOYAGE OF DISCOVERY AND ADVENTURE
by Bob Bitchin
"The refreshingly irreverent ex-biker Bob Bitchin views the high seas as another highway to ride flat-out to fun and adventure. But rather than mayhem, he finds the cruising camaraderie and respect for the sea that all voyagers share."
Caribbean Compass

THE BREATH OF ANGELS
A TRUE STORY OF LIFE AND DEATH AT SEA
by John Beattie
"A riveting, powerful, more-dramatic-than-fiction, true biographical story of life and death upon the open sea."
The Midwest Book Review

America's Favorite Sailing Books
www.sheridanhouse.com

The Mariner's Library Fiction Classics Series

AN EYE OF THE FLEET
A NATHANIEL DRINKWATER NOVEL
by Richard Woodman
This is the first book in the acclaimed Nathaniel Drinkwater series.
Action in Admiral Rodney's dramatic Moonlight Battle of 1780,
when CYCLOPS' capture of the Santa Teresa plays a decisive part, is
the start of Nathaniel Drinkwater's life at sea.

A BRIG OF WAR
A NATHANIEL DRINKWATER NOVEL
by Richard Woodman
Drinkwater's fight to bring a half-armed ship safely to the Cape of
Good Hope is beset with personal enmity, the activity of the French
and the violence of the sea.

WAGER
by Richard Woodman
Sailing his tea clipper, ERL KING, in 1869, Captain "Cracker Jack"
Kemball races Captain Richards of the SEAWITCH from Shanghai to
London. The wager: his daughter's hand in marriage.

ENDANGERED SPECIES
by Richard Woodman
Captain John Mackinnon and his ship, the MATTHEW FLINDERS,
embark on their last voyage. Their journey to Hong Kong will
prove to be anything but quiet. They encounter a typhoon, the
rescue of a boatload of Vietnamese refugees, and mutiny.

THE DARKENING SEA
by Richard Woodman
From the clash of mighty battleships at Jutland in 1916 to the cold
splendor the present day Arctic, *The Darkening Sea* traces the
fortunes of the Martin family throughout nearly seventy years of
British maritime history.

America's Favorite Sailing Books
www.sheridanhouse.com